# The RAGE of GAIN

## PATRICK CLEARY

The

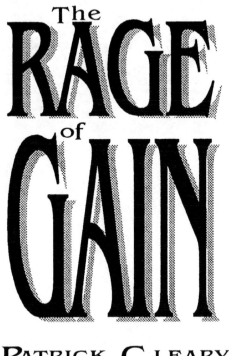

# RAGE
## of
# GAIN

PATRICK CLEARY

**Adelphi Press**
4-6 Effie Road, London SW6 1TD

Printed and bound in the UK
Published by Adelphi Press
ISBN 1 85654 101 0

*Aid slighted truth;*
*with thy persuasive strain*
*Teach erring man to spurn the rage of gain;*
*Teach him that states of native strength possess'd*
*Though very poor may still be very bless'd;*
*That trade's proud empire hastes to swift decay*
*As ocean sweeps the labour'd mole away;*
*While self-dependent power can time defy,*
*As rocks resist the billows and the sky.*

*Oliver Goldsmith.*

## Acknowledgements:

The author would like to thank Breda for her forbearance, Maura Leyden Lifford Ennis for wordprocessing, John Kelly (Clare Champion photographer), and all others who helped in any way.

# DEDICATION

For my daughter Helen

# Contents

# Chapter 1

The Dunleys were considered to be well-to-do farmers by the standards of rural Ireland of the late 1940's. John Dunley and his wife Nora had two boys with only a year or so separating their ages; they also had a daughter, Mary Kate, who was around ten years older and had long since married well, into another farm only a few miles inland as the crow flies. John was a no nonsense, God-fearing man in his late sixties from a well-respected family of land owners going back generations. In fact, he was proud that according to the local church records the Dunleys held land as far back as the records themselves. Nora, nearly twenty five years his junior, came from the other end of the county and brought with her a dowry. That was the custom of the time; the prospective bride brought a sum of money with her when marrying well. It was a "made" match, a very common occurrence of the day but it was a happy union, and they had three healthy offspring to prove it. John and Nora Dunley were hard-working people with strongly held religious convictions.

Peter was the second boy of the family, a tall, well-proportioned, handsome young lad of fair complexion and blond hair, with an artistic flair, fond of music and generally considered to be a good singer, judging by the calls on him at local parties and the Christmas concerts. He was also the boy earmarked to go to secondary school - the oldest son customarily stayed on the farm and inherited the place when the parents' finally retired. It was just as well that Peter came second of the boys because he had no interest whatever in farming and avoided it at every opportunity. That is, except for the horses which the Dunleys kept and were famed for. His father was known far and wide in the farming community for his great knowledge of the equine species and often won prizes at agricultural shows for the best-turned-out colt. Peter had taken after him and at every spare moment could be found grooming or exercising the grey mare or breaking in the young black filly. As a sensitive young man, he hated being in the vicinity at pig killing time - indeed the screams of the pig before slaughter chilled the marrow of his bones, as he later recalled. He also detested the beheading of a chicken or a goose to be prepared for the plentiful table for which the Dunleys were well known. Going off to secondary college appealed to him greatly, as he would now be getting away from the drudgery that he associated with the land. He was happy, too, to be leaving the primary school and the misery that it had become to him. In fact, he was known to have answered ''yes'' on a questionnaire, given to his class by a travelling vocations priest from some religious order, when asked if he would like to go away with them. It transpired within weeks, however, that young Peter, far from being interested in joining that particular novitiate, was merely trying to get away from, what was in later years, described by him as the tyranny of his early school days.

The Dunleys farmed around one hundred acres of mainly good land in an out of the way townland called Kilrane, three miles from the village of Killavone where it was still considered unusual, that a boy would be going away to a boarding college, but Dunley was a proud man as well as a thrifty farmer and was determined that his second son would be well educated. He was, by now, making arrangements with the local priest that Peter would go to St. Kevin's, a college of renown where vocations were fostered for the priesthood. Canon Jim Mulraney was the parish priest of Killavone, a stern, red-faced, autocratic man whose word in everything was final, but he and farmer Dunley got on well, both sharing a love of horses, and the Canon was often to be seen, particularly in the long evenings of summer, exercising his own filly on Dunley's land. Late one evening the Canon arrived on horseback with the good news that he had put in a good word with the college superiors and that Peter would be joining them in September. Nora, the boy's mother, was overjoyed at this great news and was soon on her bicycle to visit John's sister, Annie, who lived alone some distance away. She had one son living in County Wexford, called Jerome, who had been born out of wedlock and who was known to have prospered in business. He rarely came home to see her although he provided for her financially. Nora had come to tell Annie the good news that Peter was off to secondary school and with God's help would go on for the priesthood. At that time in Ireland, it was the ardent wish of every mother that she would rear a son who became a priest and many a rosary was recited for those intentions. Any pocket money that young Peter possessed was given to him by Aunt Annie as she was well aware that her brother, John, wasn't known to dole out money lavishly - the meagre few pence that he gave the boys on a Saturday were coupled with the admonition that money didn't grow on trees.

Langan's forge was a regular haunt of Peter's, particularly on wet days, and where he spent many hours observing blacksmith Mickey Langan perform his works of art with wrought iron which he rendered on a coal fire that was fanned by a bellows, operated by Langan with his left arm. Young Peter marvelled at the way a horse was shod or an iron gate was assembled in front of his eyes. Indeed, the smell of the horses hoof when the red hot shoe was applied and the white smoke that filled the forge, remained in his nostrils long after Mickey Langan was laid to rest. Peter was also friendly with the saddler, Walsh, and had often cause to visit him when a horse's saddle or bridle needed attention.

# Chapter 2

All summer long Peter looked forward to the first week in September, when he would be waving goodbye to his family and leaving home with his suitcase of possessions to start a new life in St. Kevin's.

The odd old pupil that John Dunley came across in his travels or through his enquiries from Canon Jim were duly invited to the Dunley homestead where young Peter would listen in awe to the many tales they had to tell of college life at St. Kevin's and the friendships that he would establish and, in some cases, cement for life with boys from many different walks of life. He was starry-eyed in anticipation of it all but he also knew that he would be lonely leaving the family home. It was a long time between terms, when he would be having his first break from school. However, there was now much else to think about and feelings such as loneliness would have to be shelved.

Peter Dunley had barely acclimatised himself to college life when he had a rude awakening. He was now expected to rise at 5.45 am, observe silence, wash, dress, make his bed and get to the college chapel in thirty minutes flat. There, he was introduced to what was to become the ritual of morning prayers and daily mass - followed by a period of study before a very meagre breakfast, only after which could silence be broken. Each student took the same position each morning in the chapel and in the college refectory, and he soon came to realise that he was now obliged to conform in the same way as Dunley's forty cows did each morning when they lined up in their own places for milking.

In no time at all Peter was conforming to this strict routine and becoming a model student. The friendship he struck up with Paddy Morrissey had a lot to do with shaping his attitudes. Paddy was athletic, good at sports, and played the piano. He was also a very religious boy and had his sights firmly set on the priesthood. They became firm friends and Peter often recalled that that was what Canon Jim must have meant when he told him that friendships were cemented in college. His parents were delighted with the lovely young man, as Nora described him, whom Peter brought to stay at the Dunley homestead during school holidays. Peter was now seventeen and was allowed to accompany his older brother, Joe, to a dance in the local village hall. It was there that he was introduced to a young lady of similar age, called Rosaleen. From the moment they laid eyes on each other, the world seemed to stand still for both of them. Rosaleen was an attractive girl, petite, with long blonde hair that would have reached her waist were it not that she had tied it into two identical plaits on either side of her face. She had beautiful blue eyes, perfectly chiselled features and lips that Peter couldn't take his eyes off. He asked her to dance, his heart pounding so fiercely that he imagined people would actually hear it around the hall. They moved to the dance floor and he held her awkwardly at first until they both got into the tempo of the music, holding each other at a respectful distance until the demands of the music forced Peter to draw her more closely to him. Did she feel his heart pounding he wondered - was she enjoying it as much as he was? He hoped the music would never end, but end it did when the band leader ended Peter's ecstasy abruptly with the announcement of the next dance of the evening. During the dance with Rosaleen, he had determined that she had come from a neighbouring parish some five or six miles west of Killavone. Would he meet her again before the evening was over? Who was the tall, dark fellow now dancing with her for the second time? He swapped notes with his brother, Joe, who was standing at the back of the crowded, smoke-filled hall. Joe was able to put Peter out of his misery by informing him that the dark-haired stranger was none other than Rosaleen's brother, who had escorted her to the dance. He asked her to dance again, and plucking up courage, asked her for a date. To his delight, she said ''yes'' and they arranged to meet on the following Wednesday night in a country lane with a graveyard as a landmark not far from her home. The excitement was only just beginning for Peter. How would he get away from home, he thought? He had no transport. He could hardly saddle up the grey mare and ride there at the dead of night. Besides, John Dunley would have stabled the horses at that time and it was highly unlikely that he wouldn't hear the clatter of the horse's hooves on the courtyard next to the house. Peter decided that he would take his mother's bicycle from the shed. He discussed the matter with his brother and his visitor, Paddy Morrissey, who were both sworn to secrecy about his escapade.

The meeting took place at the appointed time with the lovely Rosaleen, who was waiting in the lane, with her brother acting as chaperon. They nervously walked hand in hand, away from him down the dark lane, clutching each other tightly, embracing and finally kissing - the very first time for both of them. He feverishly pressed her lips to his and held them there longingly, he pulled her close to him and she made feeble attempts to extricate herself and then she seemed to relax. Soon it was time to part because the brother was signalling that he was getting restless. The time had slipped by so rapidly, and now they were saying goodbye again but they vowed before parting that they would meet again during the Easter holidays. They declared their mutual love. Peter parted from his Rosaleen with tears welling in his eyes.

# Chapter 3

Peter Dunley found that time seemed to be accelerating, hurtling him towards his final examinations. He had seen the College vocations director on a couple of occasions, regarding his future, and despite his fondness for Rosaleen, with whom he corresponded secretly through letters forwarded via his sister Mary Kate, he felt that he had a vocation for the Priesthood. Rosaleen, too, was entering her final year in secondary school and was undecided what she would do. She thought that she might sit the Civil Service Examination if her results were good enough.

It was final count-down time for Peter and his friend, Paddy Morrissey, as their interview approached with the College President that would decide their fate. Many of their friends were entering the Novitiate and they, too, felt that the time had come for them to decide. John and Nora, together with Auntie Annie, had come to visit Peter in his final month at St. Kevin's to be told by the College Superiors that he was indeed going on for the priesthood. They were ecstatic; Nora's prayers were answered and she visualised him in clerical black attire coming home on his holidays each term until he would be finally ordained, and as Aunt Annie observed he had the makings of a lovely priest; tall, handsome and so pious!

During the summer vacation, while he awaited the results of his final exams, that would copperfasten his entry to the Seminary, he decided to have his final fling, as Langan the blacksmith called it, every time he spotted young Peter with the lovely Rosaleen. Peter had by now introduced her to his close friends around Killavone and had a standing invitation to take her to tea to his sister, Mary Kate's, as often as they liked. Nearly everyone had met Rosaleen by now except John and Nora Dunley, who, he was well aware would not have approved that a young man about to enter the Religious life would be company keeping. That was the term used for courting couples at that time in rural Ireland. They were confirmed in their view to keep well clear of the parents after they had accidentally run into Auntie Annie near the Post Office, who quickly got on her bicycle without acknowledging their greeting and cycled down the hill out of view. They were philosophical about it though - after all wouldn't he soon be locked up again, this time in a stricter regime and wasn't he only having his final fling as Mickey Langan had told him?

Canon Jim Mulraney had a different view of things though, as he told Peter in no uncertain terms when he observed "the two lovebirds" as he described them, holding hands as they sat on the bridge below the village. He summoned them both to his study in the Parochial House, a rambling six-bedroomed, two-storey residence in its own grounds in the centre of Killavone. What transpired at that meeting left Peter and his Rosaleen in no doubt that they should end the relationship forthwith. As Canon Jim bellowed at them "It was unheard of to be company keeping and giving a bad example to the other Parishioners." It would be more appropriate, he thundered, if Peter were to ponder on the vows of chastity and obedience which he would soon have to take in the Novitiate. That traumatic meeting was enough for poor Rosaleen who tearfully left the priest's house and hurried away from Killavone, vowing that she would wipe the memory of her lovely Peter forever from her mind.

# Chapter 4

Peter and his friend, Paddy, arranged to meet at the Railway Station that would take them and their worldly belongings to "Broadlands", a huge stone-built, austere-looking edifice situated in thirty acres at the Northern end of the country. The property had been donated to the Church Authorities a half century earlier by a wealthy Catholic peer who died without leaving an heir. The total estate of four hundred and fifty acres was now owned by Lord Dunglory but the house and acreage were shelved off for the Novitiate which had by now been awarded University status.

Peter and Paddy were met at the station by a tall, lanky, balding priest dressed in a long cassock. They had already noticed him pacing up and down the station platform as they looked from their carriage of the train that was jolting to a stop at Kinlare Station. They waited their turn to collect their belongings, comprising of two battered suitcases, before he approached them and introduced himself as Fr. Talbot, their Dean of Studies. "Broadlands" was a mere thirty minutes walk from there he advised them and the walk would do them good after such a long train journey! The other students, he remarked, had long since arrived and should be well settled in to their allotted rooms by now. As they walked up the driveway that led to the entrance to the Novitiate, they heard a bell tolling which, they were told, signalled the call for prayers in the chapel before they retired for the night. The boys were ravenous with hunger after the long train journey and were quickly realising what self denial would mean. There was the consolation that they were sharing the same accommodation. Life at the Novitiate was similar to the

College life that they had experienced except that they would be treated more like adults from now on. It wasn't all about religion either, they came to appreciate; there were the Lectures in English Literature, Classical Studies, Continental Languages, Psychology, Philosophy and Theology. They particularly liked the classes of an elderly cleric called Father Paul whose forte was Hagiology, or the study of the Saints. Fr. Paul was unique in that he seemed to deliver his gems of wisdom with his eyes firmly closed. He was a heavy smoker too, (even though tobacco was rationed at that time), judging by his nicotine-stained fingers and teeth. He had a peculiar habit, they observed, of chewing cloves which older seminarians knew were a good antidote to the odd drop of liquor to which he was partial.

Towards the end of his third term at "Broadlands" Peter received a visit from his sister Mary Kate and her new-born baby which she asked him to bless for her. She had christened her Nora after their mother. She also had something special for Peter - it was an important envelope with Rosaleen's handwriting which he recognised the moment she took it from her handbag. He hurriedly opened it to find a photograph of her, together with a letter. They made their way around the walks that skirted the flower beds of the beautiful, landscaped gardens at the front of the Novitiate. He read the contents as they walked along. The letter ran as follows:

*My dear Peter,*

*It seems an eternity since that dreadful last evening together in Canon Mulraney's study. How I hated that man for what he did to us, but you have decided dear Peter, that your future is in the Church. I think of you often and I hope that you spare a thought for me sometimes. I am giving this letter to Mary Kate to take to you when she visits you. She is lovely and understanding to me. You won't be able to be seen with me any longer now that you will be wearing your clerical black suits when you come home on holidays. Your mother would be very cross with me if she knew that I had written to you. I'm sending you this photograph which was taken at school and I hope that you will think of me when you look at it. I got the Civil Service job and will be off to Dublin at the beginning of January but you will be home before I go away. God bless you and I can say I love you even though it's not right for me to say this to you now. Goodbye, dear Peter - from your loving*

*Rosaleen.*

At the end of his sister's visit, Peter waved farewell to her and went straight up to his room where he hid the letter in the mattress after re-reading its contents. He had never prayed so hard for guidance as he did that night that he would, eventually, forget Rosaleen. He put the photograph in his breast pocket and looked at it often. He thought she looked lovely and was exactly how he remembered her from that first night he laid eyes on her in the local hall at Killavone. He talked at length about her with his room-mate Paddy who advised him that he should discuss his problems with his confessor. Peter concurred after Paddy had reminded him that she was only a friend now. The confessor agreed with his friend's view of the matter, leaving Peter more confident about his vocation. During that Christmas holiday he never laid eyes on Rosaleen and spent the Festive Season quietly with his parents. He was settling down at last he felt.

# Chapter 5

Rosaleen wasn't long in Dublin when she met an attractive young man - not unlike Peter, but a city type who was fond of the bright lights. He swept her off her feet in a matter of a few months and thoughts of Peter seemed to fade into oblivion. She was now helplessly in love with her new fellow, she told Mary Kate in a letter, and they would probably be getting married when she was twenty-one years old. Her parents would not hear of it before then, she told her. They weren't engaged or anything like that and he hadn't asked her but she knew that he would do so given time. She had decided, she told Mary Kate in the letter, that she would take him to meet Peter in the Seminary. Mary Kate duly wrote to Peter advising him of the impending visit so that he would be prepared for them.

He was looking out of the study hall window facing the main gate of "Broadlands" when he saw a black motorcar come up the driveway. He was filled with barely suppressed rage when he saw who alighted from the vehicle. It was his Rosaleen with her new boyfriend. She was looking really beautiful as they made their way to the front door of the college. Wearing his favourite pink, she walked hand in hand down the hall with her man and enquired at the desk for Peter. He went out to meet them his emotions in turmoil.

"Hello Peter, how are you? This is my new boyfriend James - isn't he lovely? I thought you should be the very first to meet him," she blurted out all at once. Peter stared at him for some moments and merely said "How do you do James?" He was immaculately dressed in a well-fitting double breasted check suit with white shirt and silk tie - Peter in contrast was wearing his everyday shabby soutane. Rosaleen told Peter that James was not a Catholic but would be taking instruction in the Faith before they announced their engagement and when the time came she wanted Peter to be at the wedding. James, she said, had a magnificent job as a Chartered Accountant for a very large company and would soon be promoted by his firm. Soon the Novitiate bell rang for study which released Peter from his visit. He bade them farewell and rushed to his room where he threw himself on his bed and sobbed bitterly. That night he could not sleep with thoughts of Rosaleen and James. He knew that it wasn't right to have thoughts of this nature but the more he prayed the more obsessed he became about them, only now, his thoughts were different. He looked at the clock on the wall and wondered what they were doing together. Were they living together he wondered - could they be sleeping together? He tortured himself with visions of them and looked at her photograph which he gazed at until he felt he could almost touch her. He lay with his hands behind his head and was sure that he could see her image on the ceiling, lying in an embrace with James. Paddy shook him awake at 6 am - it was time to get up for morning prayers and Mass. That morning he listened intently to the preacher's sermon on the vow of chastity. "Every healthy young man," he said, "was subject to fantasies about the opposite sex. This was quite normal," he went on, "as long as one did not fantasise too much and thereby take pleasure in it. That," he concluded, "would be committing sins of the mind and body - sins of the flesh which broke the vow of chastity." Peter felt reassured that he was quite normal but he was starting to realise also that it wasn't just Rosaleen that he fantasised about, but other beautiful women also. On examining his conscience, for example, he vividly recalled the well-dressed lady who visited

one of the seminarians regularly and who smelled so excitingly
of a particular fragrance that it almost overwhelmed him when
he brushed past her - and was it his imagination that she often
glanced to him too he wondered?

# Chapter 6

Peter Dunley had by now endured over four years of seminary life and had grown accustomed to the rigours that a vocation brought with it. He was pronounced an Acolyte and was assumed to be well on his way to final ordination of Holy Orders. He was going to town freely and helping out in the parishes around the area where he mixed with the local populace. He walked a lot, found it hard to concentrate on prayer but tired nevertheless. One morning he was at Mass in the local town for the repose of the soul of a friend's mother when a strikingly beautiful woman entered the same pew and knelt beside him. He buried his face in his hands in an effort to blot her from his mind but the more he did so, the more he was consumed by a wild passion in his body. He decided to leave the church and on making his exit from the pew, had to brush past this beautiful woman. She had stood up to let him pass and he distinctly felt her body rub against his before he hurried from the church. After the Mass, he watched her leave the church grounds only this time he knew it was much different - he looked at her in a way that he knew he shouldn't. In fact he mentally undressed her and wanted her with a passion that he never even dreamt of with Rosaleen. It was time for him to get out - he was convinced. That night he lay awake pondering his future and planning an escape from a building that had now become his prison.

Peter Dunley had decided that, he would not tell a soul of his intention to leave the Priesthood at the first opportunity - not even his good friend and room-mate, Paddy. A way had to be found urgently, to leave "Broadlands" without attracting attention to himself; he made a careful note of the comings and goings of delivery men, Post Office vans and a large vehicle that arrived at the Seminary weekly with groceries and vegetables. This, he felt, was his chance to escape unnoticed, by jumping into the back of the vehicle after the empty returns were collected by the driver at the back of the college. He decided to make a break for it with just the clothes he was wearing together with an old raincoat which he found on the floor of the vehicle. The van travelled for what seemed like an hour when the driver appeared to pull into a yard where he alighted and entered a building. This was Peter's chance to escape and he took the opportunity without hesitation. He donned the old raincoat and walked briskly down a country road to his left, before crossing a cornfield until he came to a crossroads. He continued straight on, walking at a steady pace along country lanes until night fell and he was exhausted, cold and hungry. He was about to investigate the possibility of resting for the night in an old haybarn at the side of the road when he spotted a tiny farmhouse across the fields where he thought he saw a light flickering in the window. He made his way across some fences towards the little house when a white sheepdog came darting towards him, barking furiously. As he was about to knock on the farmhouse door, it opened suddenly and an elderly man appeared carrying an oil lamp. He called the dog in and enquired of Peter what his business was. He noticed that the old man was clutching a rosary beads in his right hand. The barking of the dog at the corner of the house had interrupted their night prayers - this was a popular ritual at that time in rural Ireland where families recited the Rosary before retiring for the night. As he entered, a kindly old lady beckoned Peter to kneel by a chair and recite a decade when it came to his turn.

When the prayers were finished the old lady enquired graciously as to Peter's business. He was reticent about telling them his story at first and merely remarked that he had lost his way. "What state of hunger are you in?" enquired the old woman as she filled the large, black kettle and hung it on a crane over the open fire. She then went to the cupboard and produced a fine sliver of bacon and home-made bread and made the tea. Peter pulled up to the table and laid into what was his first bite of food that day. After the old man had gone to bed, Peter took the old lady into his confidence about what he intended to do if she would kindly help him.

Telephones were still very scarce in those days, but Peter knew that his cousin Jerome Dunley in Wexford had one, and his plan was to make contact with him as soon as possible. Jerome was Peter's cousin and the son of Auntie Annie, John Dunley's sister. He had been born out of wedlock, had never known his own father and had been given the Dunley surname. Jerome was now a wealthy businessman, drove a smart motorcar and lived in a fabulous house on the outskirts of the town and enjoyed life in the fast lane. He was married to an attractive French woman whom Peter had met only once when he came to Killavone and spent money lavishly on the locals in each of the three public houses in the village. He was known as the well-off Dunley boy although nobody seemed to know what exactly Jerome did for a living or how he had come to make so much money - but he was wealthy; of this they had no doubt.

# Chapter 7

Peter was taken in the pony and trap by the old lady the following morning after a breakfast of boiled eggs and brown bread washed down by two large mugs of strong tea, and not before she had provided him with a change of clothing for his journey - they were her nephew's working clothes she said, consisting of grey flannel trousers and a pullover that was a bit on the big side for him. Peter was grateful to be discarding the black attire which he folded neatly and deposited in the hayshed at the back of the house. She took him to a railway station where she knew a man on the staff, who helped them get Jerome Dunley's telephone number; it wasn't difficult as it transpired because Dunley Enterprises was listed more than once in the telephone book.

Before the kindly old lady bade farewell and good luck to Peter, she paid the clerk for the telephone call and gave Peter a few shillings to purchase a train ticket and generally tide him over until he made contact with the cousins. He vowed that the kindness he had received from the farmhouse couple would not be forgotten.

A lady called Monique answered Peter's telephone call. "This is Monique Dunley," she said, "who is this?" "Is your husband there?" Peter enquired, and before he could say who he was, a male voice came on the line and said "Jerome Dunley here, can I help you?" "This is Peter - eh, your cousin Peter .... Dunley....your uncle John's son." "How are you Peter? - where are you? --- shouldn't I be calling you Father by now?" he joked. "I'm calling you from a railway station in the middle of County Louth - it's a long story, Jerome, that I would prefer to discuss with you face to face,'' said Peter. ''I would like to visit you as soon as possible because I am in a spot of bother.'' Jerome was exceptionally understanding and gave him directions on how to get to County Wexford from Drogheda - a journey of several hours he warned. He left the telephone and returned with the instructions that there was a train for Dublin at 11.30 am and he would get a connection from there at 3.45 pm - arriving in Wexford town at approximately 8 pm that evening. ''I will be there to meet you,'' said Jerome. ''I look forward to it very much and thank you,'' said Peter gratefully. From the moment he replaced the receiver he felt an enormous sense of freedom even though he knew that it wouldn't be easy for him to come to terms with all the problems facing him. There was the scandal of fleeing the seminary without informing anyone; he couldn't contact his parents for obvious reasons - he worried greatly about the effect it would have on his family, particularly his parents, when they heard the news.

Peter enjoyed the train journey and for much of the time had a carriage all to himself. He observed the various passengers as they came and went about their business. The scenery was magnificent as the train made its way through the country, pulling into all the rural stations en route. It was only his second time in a train; the first was with his friend Paddy Morrissey on their way to start life in ''Broadlands'' Ecclesiastical Seminary. He wondered what Paddy was thinking now. It was so unfair of him not to tell him of his intention to leave....but he would be in touch as soon as he sorted himself out.

His cousin, Jerome Dunley and lovely wife, Monique, were waiting on the platform as the train finally drew into the station. The clock read 8.15 pm as Peter alighted from his carriage and walked towards them. They seemed very happy to be meeting him. Monique enquired whether he was collecting his luggage from the train, a question that met with a startled expression on Peter's face. She quickly realised that all was not well and that explanations could follow later. Jerome had already opened the doors of his limousine for Monique and Peter and they began the short journey to their home on the outskirts of the town. He was most understanding, as details of Peter's decision to abandon the Priesthood, and his current plight, unfolded. They both agreed that, taking all the circumstances into account, he had acted wisely; perhaps, Jerome added, he should have advised the authorities at the college before leaving but in the main he had acted wisely. Monique agreed that time was a great healer and would sort out everything. Their home-help summoned them to the dining room after Peter had enjoyed the luxury of a hot bath and shave and he settled into a meal, the likes of which he had never before experienced. It was Friday night.

# Chapter 8

Canon Jim Mulraney was knocking on John Dunley's door at Kilrane as the family were getting up to attend to the morning's milking. He had just received an urgent message from the President of "Broadlands" College that Peter had not reported for study and had not spent the night in his room and must now be presumed missing. The Gardai would have to be notified he said, if the family did not know of his whereabouts. John Dunley was thunderstryck, and his wife Nora had to be helped to a chair, to combat the shock. Where was he? John Dunley went to the cupboard and pulled out a bottle of whiskey. He poured a full glass and handed it to the Canon. "How could he do this to us?", he grunted, as he grabbed the glass and emptied the contents down his throat in one go. "What are the people going to make of this when they hear that he has broken his vows?", he enquired, as he returned the glass to Dunley to repeat the dose. Nora was the person who needed the drink, she was so shocked, but she had never touched alcohol in his life and had hoped that the children would follow in her footsteps. John took a drop only at Christmas or maybe when a special occasion demanded, but he always kept a bottle of 'Paddy' in case the Canon or some other important person called at the house. They stayed talking about the situation concerning Peter for an hour or so and just as the Canon was about to leave, the postman came up the path clutching a telegram. He seemed excited as if he already knew the contents of the message. Dunley grabbed the envelope and tore it open nervously, reading the message with incredulity. He repeated it aloud to his audience.

*WEXFORD P.O.*

*Peter is here and safe....stop....He will not be returning to the Novitiate....stop....Inform the Canon and "Broadlands"....stop....JEROME.*

As if he hadn't heard correctly the first time, Canon Jim grabbed the telegram from John and muttered the contents to himself several times...."I don't know what the world is coming to," he growled. Poor Nora was in tears as she rose from her chair. "I'm glad he's alright," she sobbed,...."no one cared about that...did ye?" She repeated it and walked slowly out of the kitchen and proceeded to the milking parlour to start her day's work.

# Chapter 9

Jerome Dunley spent much time away from home due to his business commitments while Monique stayed at home to keep an eye on their local interests. They had been living together nearly ten years but had no children. She liked Peter a lot and was delighted that he had settled in so well. She drove him to town and advised him on the purchase of clothing; she then took him to the town's best barber where he had his hair styled and groomed, and before long was remarking that he looked like a film star. They went out to lunch, visited the cinema, had drinks in the local hotels where she introduced Peter to her wide circle of friends. Jerome telephoned often; he was in England at present and would be going to Germany afterwards to an Exhibition. Monique told Peter how much she enjoyed his company in Jerome's absence. She reminded him often how handsome he was and hoped that he could stay with them indefinitely. Peter was very flattered by her comments and was secretly very enamoured with her and often wondered how he could convey his feelings. Monique was a delightful-looking woman in her early thirties, a tall statuesque red-head with a sallow complexion, and quite stunning when she wore her black blouse and tight green skirt. It was the revealing blouse that Peter found so appealing when they sat down opposite each other to dine. She was going to bed early, she told him because she was taking him to Dublin on the following day. After dinner, they sat together in the drawing room where she poured out drinks. Peter was beginning to enjoy the occasional glass of Guinness or, better still, the gin and tonics to which she had introduced him. She played some of her favourite records and they danced. Peter whispered to her that he was very happy, and she asked if he liked her perfume. She was wearing it just for him, she said. She pressed herself closer and he could feel her tremble as she moved her body to the rhythm of the music. Her hair was touching his face as he gently kissed her neck....soon their lips met and they kissed....ever so gently at first until he seemed to feel her tongue....it drove him crazy....he thought momentarily of Rosaleen but now knew that this was not the way they had kissed that night near the graveyard....Monique let him touch her breasts....he was going out of his mind with desire. How could he cope with it as Monique opened her blouse further and allowed his lips to kiss her nipples? She was breathing heavily and her body was writhing as she seemed to go limp in his arms - he walked backwards as they continued kissing and fondling each other, stumbling across furniture until they fell headlong onto the settee. There she untied the belt of his trousers and opened his shirt buttons....she tugged at the shirt and she took him by the hand and led him up the stairs, items of their clothing scattering along the way until they were both naked. She took him to the master bedroom where he laid her down on the giant four-posted bed....he caressed her all over and they made love...he, for the first time in his life....When morning came, Peter full of remorse, wanted to leave but she persuaded him to stay, telling him that there was no need to worry - she would never tell her husband.

When Jerome finally returned from Europe, he was surprised that Peter was still there and advised him that he would have to find a job appropriate to his education. He couldn't stay with them forever. Peter agreed and told Monique that he would have to go. He felt that he was cheating on his cousin who had provided him with shelter when he badly needed it and fed and clothed him when he was desperate. He told Jerome that he would look for a job and move out to find a suitable place for himself. Jerome assented.

Peter was now preoccupied with the feeling that he must see his family and was making arrangements to go to Kilrane when a letter arrived for him from his mother. It read:

*Kilrane,*
*Killavone P.O.*

*Dearest Peter,*

*You have hurt us greatly but particularly your father who has not been well since we received the sad news that you are not, after all, going on for the priesthood. Please come and see us soon. Joe and Mary Kate would love to see you too. Have you got a job? How are you off for money? Auntie Annie has been enquiring about you. Please write and let us know when you are coming to see us. Your father is ill and anxious to see you.*

*Love from your Mammy.*

# Chapter 10

John Dunley was just turned seventy when he passed away peacefully, with his wife Nora and all three children around his bed. Just before he died, he clasped Peter tightly by the hand and whispered "Welcome home, son." He then turned over on his side and closed his eyes for the last time. Peter knelt down by the bedside still holding his father's hand and prayed for the first time since finishing the rosary with the old couple in the farmhouse on his first night of freedom from the Novitiate.

Jerome and Monique had accompanied Peter home and were relieved that they were there for the funeral. At that time in rural Ireland, there was a 'wake' held in the home of the person who had died as Funeral Parlours did not come into fashion until much later. All the relatives and neighbours from the parish and beyond came to pay their last respects and were treated to as much alcohol as they were able to consume, as well as high tea during the night. Many of them stayed with the corpse until daybreak when they went home to attend to their farming duties prior to the funeral. John Dunley's funeral was like that and locals were heard to observe that the likes of the crowd that attended his burial had never been seen in the parish before, so vast was it. He was buried in the family vault out at the old graveyard at Kilrane where generations of the Dunleys were interred. On the day he was laid to rest, Nora was just forty-five years of age. Peter visited all his relatives and friends after his father's burial and then decided that he would return to Wexford with Jerome and Monique. He felt that there was nothing in Killavone to interest him anymore. He had grown away from it and was now preoccupied with carving out a life of his own, in a manner he hoped would emulate Jerome's life style. He felt that he would probably never have his wealth but he craved the affluence to which he and Monique had introduced him.

# Chapter 11

Clark Beswell and his wife Catherine were a very wealthy couple who lived in a huge mansion on a considerable estate about thirty miles from Wexford town. They were both in their early forties and owned the famous Kerrigart Stud which was renowned for some of the finest bred racehorses in Ireland or the Continent.

Monique had just received a telephone call from Catherine saying that they were holding a dinner party and would like it if Jerome and herself could come along. Monique accepted the invitation but explained that they had a house guest at present, a cousin of Jerome's. "Please bring him along with you," said Catherine, "we shall be delighted to meet him." The friendship between the two families had grown since Clark and Jerome had met during a golf tournament between their companies. They were both low handicap golfers and met often in the Club. They and their wives got on very well together.

When Peter heard from Monique about the invitation, he was overjoyed. Everyone had heard of the Beswells and the Kerrigart Stud, he told her and couldn't believe his luck to be about to mingle with so many influential people from the equine world. He wished that his father was still alive because he knew that he would have been greatly impressed. Monique had heard from Peter of his great love of horses, and now he had the opportunity of meeting like-minded people.

Catherine Beswell was an English girl and a gifted musician and arranger. She had come to Ireland just out of Music School to produce a show for the Orpheus Musical Society, met Clark there and fell in love with him. She later came back and married him. Clark's parents had been in business in Ireland since the 1800's, originally a Canadian family; they had amassed great wealth but had now returned to their roots leaving Clark to further develop his bloodstock interests in Leinster. He was developing a sizeable business in the export of thoroughbreds to the European Continent and the Arab world. Since Catherine had married him, she had also taken a great interest in horses and was often to be seen riding with the Hounds or exercising young thoroughbreds on their nearly thousand acre Estate.

When Jerome, Monique and Peter entered the Beswell demesne from the Gate Lodge, Peter was reminded of "Broadlands", the Seminary where he finally broke his vows and fled to what was now his new-found freedom.

Catherine received them at the entrance, a tall, dark, elegant lady in her early forties, dressed excitingly in a stunning gown complemented by expensive jewellery. Peter was simply bowled over by her appearance and demeanour. She was warm and friendly, he thought, when Monique introduced them to one another. She kissed him on the cheek by way of welcome. Then it was Jerome's turn - they embraced and kissed full on the lips, Peter noticed. Monique had already entered and was being met in the hall by Clark Beswell. A member of the household staff took their coats and they were escorted to the Drawing Room by Catherine and introduced to the other guests already present. Peter looked aghast at the decor, furnishings and general opulence of the room. The outside driveway and house structure may have reminded him of "Broadlands" but that was where the similarity ended, he thought. After drinks, a bell rang to summon the guests to the dining room hall where dinner was about to be served. They had thought of everything - even the menus were specially printed for the occasion, emblazoned with the Beswell family crest. Peter yearned for this style of living - now he knew how the other half lived he wished to be part of it. When the guests sat down to dine, he noticed the pecking order, judging by the guests seated nearest the hosts. He fantasised about what he would have discussed with the lovely Catherine had he been placed next to her. As it happened, Jerome and Monique were nearest the top of the table and Catherine sat opposite them. Peter was pleasantly surprised to have his smile returned by Catherine whose gaze seemed to linger on him, and her attention flattered him. As the brandies were being served, the orchestra provided for the guests' entertainment could he heard tuning up in an adjoining room. Peter entered with Monique and was soon on the dance floor with her. The other couples followed while Catherine and Clark conversed with a number of unaccompanied guests, the local vicar and two elderly ladies who, judging by their demeanour, had helped themselves liberally to somebody's drinks cabinet. "Are you enjoying the party?" Monique enquired of her dancing partner who replied that he was grateful for the invitation and was having a great time. "You look the most handsome man here," she continued, as she held herself closely to Peter. "I think you are looking fabulous tonight and I love your dress," he said. "What do you think of Catherine? She is quite beautiful, isn't she?" "I hadn't really thought about her", said Peter, telling a blatant lie as she was constantly on his thoughts since they first met. "Jerome seems to be paying her a lot of attention," he teased Monique. "Everybody pays Catherine lots of attention - she demands that from her men friends," snapped Monique. Peter thought better of continuing with that line of conversation. The dance ended and he escorted her to the table where Jerome was seated in the company of Clark and Catherine. "Peter, isn't it?,'' Clark enquired. ''I would like a word or two with you this evening about something - tell you what old chap, why don't we pop in to the drawing room for a chat?'' Peter was astonished. Surely, he thought, he couldn't be reading his thoughts that he fancied the lovely Catherine. They excused themselves and went through the double doors that led to an annexe of the drawing room. ''Will you have a drink, Peter? I am pleasantly surprised to hear that you are a pretty good judge of a horse.'' Before Peter could reply he went on ''You know that horses are my business - big business at that? I understand from Jerome that you are out of work at present. Didn't choose the right vocation, eh?'' he teased. ''I may have something to interest you at the Kerrigart Stud. Nothing major to start with, do you understand....general supervision of the stable lads and grooming and exercising....that kind of thing.'' Peter was speechless....''Thank you, Mr. Beswell''....''Clark will do....I must tell you that everyone here is on first name terms....dedication is the criterion by which I judge people,'' Clark replied. Peter thanked him for the offer of a job and said that he would give it his best shot....it was after all the subject nearest his heart....looking after horses. ''Fine - come over to Kerrigart on Monday morning and I'll show you around....after that I shall be out of the country so it is important that you are introduced to the workers before I go. By the way....there is a self-contained apartment above one of the stables if you don't mind sleeping with the horses'', he laughed. ''My wife Catherine will always be on hand while I'm away....be careful though young man....she is harder to handle than the wildest horse on the estate,'' he roared with laughter. After this encounter, they returned to the dance, Peter still reeling from the job offer and the conversation generally. He suddenly felt that he had known Clark Beswell all his life, he was so friendly towards him. When they returned to Jerome's table he had just got up to dance with Monique....Catherine caught Peter's hand and escorted him on to the dance floor. They danced closely, barely speaking to each other except when Catherine enquired as to the nature of his conversation with her husband. Peter told her that he had just had an offer of a job from her husband and that he had gladly accepted. "Have you, now?" said Catherine and drew herself closer to him for the remainder of the dance. After the orchestra had finished, most of the guests went home, leaving a few close friends to continue the festivities. It was Catherine's turn to show off her talents. She sat at the grand piano and gave a virtuoso performance from her vast repertoire - she gave them what they requested. 'The Pirates of Penzance' got an airing as did many others of Gilbert & Sullivan's popular pieces. She told her invited guests that her forthcoming Show with the Orpheus Musical Society would more than likely be the Rodgers & Hammerstein newly popular 'Oklahoma' and she invited her guests to consider joining the Show. When she called on a singer to give a rendition, Peter slowly got to his feet and approached her at the piano. They looked through her vast collection of sheet music before deciding on a couple of old favourites. He listened carefully to her beautiful accompaniment and introduction before singing one of his favourite songs called 'The Old Refrain', an old sentimental ballad of German origin. His crisp, clear tenor voice held the guests spellbound and they were soon on their feet calling 'encore'. Catherine was generous in her praise of her new 'discovery' and told her friends that she hoped it was only the beginning of many musical evenings together.

# Chapter 12

Peter was glowing with a combination of the drinks consumed throughout the night, his offer of a job with the Beswells, and the attention that Catherine had paid him. At 2.30 am the remainder of the guests bade their hosts good night as did Jerome, Monique and himself. Monique never spoke throughout the journey home and it was just as well, because Peter who was seated beside her in the back seat of the car, fell soundly asleep until they arrived home. He then went straight to his room, pulled off his clothes, and threw himself on the bed where he fell fast asleep.

Jerome was up early for work and Peter did not waken until he heard the telephone ringing in the hall. It was noon and Monique got to it first. He overheard some of the conversation and determined that it was Catherine at the other end of the line. When Monique finally put down the telephone she called to Peter...."Have you gone back to bed? - would you like some coffee?" He came down the stairs and into the kitchen where Monique was preparing some toast. She was clad in a flimsy negligee that revealed most of her voluptuous body. Peter entered wearing a pair of briefs and his socks....nothing more. He embraced her and tried to kiss her. She promptly pushed him away. "I don't have to ask how you enjoyed yourself last night," she snapped "the way you monopolised Catherine all evening." "Monopolised - what do you mean Monique?" "She monopolised me, you mean." "That was her on the telephone just now - she is calling in shortly on her way to town," Monique said. "For God's sake get dressed before she arrives....on second thoughts, don't bother because she'll have them off you before you know it....Be careful Peter - I'm warning you - she is a man eater.'' Peter didn't answer but shrugged his shoulders and ran upstairs to his room where he quickly put on a shirt, trousers and cardigan - the ones that Monique had chosen for him the week before. He was confused....never had he realised that he could create such interest in the opposite sex and it excited him greatly. Right now his thoughts were on the beautiful Catherine.

Peter was looking out of the bedroom window when he spotted a car coming up the drive - it was Catherine. She drove right up to the main entrance, looking ravishing, he thought, in a brightly coloured, patterned dress and head scarf. She rang the door bell and he heard Monique greet her. ''Just in time for coffee - come right in,'' she called to her. He had now gone to the bathroom to wash and shave and could hear snatches of their conversation in the kitchen. He didn't appear until he heard his name being called from the bottom of the stairs. ''Are you coming down to say hello, or shall I come up....are you decent?'' Peter emerged from the bathroom half shaven and with a towel around his shoulders....''Good morning Catherine,'' he said, with a broad smile. He walked slowly down to where she was standing on the second step. She made no attempt to move out of his way and neither did he want her to. She fell into his arms and they kissed each other meaningfully. Monique was standing by the kitchen entrance sipping her coffee and made no comment.

''This young man has the makings of a fine singer - I will have to train him for the stage,'' Catherine said, admiring him while still in his arms. ''Thank you,'' said Peter. ''I really enjoyed your party - what a wonderful musician you are....I loved your accompaniments to my songs.'' He seemed totally captivated by her. They both walked to the kitchen. ''Did he tell you that Clark has offered him a job at Kerrigart?" she asked Monique. "First I've heard of it - when do you commence?" Peter was very embarrassed that he had not told Monique about his wonderful offer. "I was about to tell you, Monique," he stammered...."yes, it's a great offer with free accommodation....I start next Tuesday after I have moved in to the apartment." Catherine told him that she would make arrangements that the Estate Manager, Matt Riordan would transfer his belongings there first. Monique smiled wryly knowing that the sum total of Peter's belongings was one suitcase of clothes which she had purchased for him since he came to live with them, the remainder of his possessions having been forwarded from "Broadlands" to his parents home at Kilrane.

# Chapter 13

Peter and Monique found themselves alone again on the eve of his departure to his new found employment with the Beswells. They had several drinks in the local hotel that evening in the absence of Jerome who had gone away again. They had dinner before returning to her house where Peter was collecting his belongings to prepare for his departure in the morning. She invited him to sleep with her and when they had undressed and got into bed, she told him that she did not want to lose him now that he was moving out of her home. "You don't have to go," she said. "I could drive you to the Stud each morning and collect you at night." Peter said that it would not work out and besides, this was a great opportunity for him to have his own apartment and the independence that it brought with it. He was physically attracted to Monique but was happy to be leaving as he didn't want any further complications, particularly as Jerome was family. They made love several times during the night and as he arose exhausted the following morning he vowed to himself that it would be their last intimate moments together.

Clark Beswell's Estate Manager arrived early as arranged by Catherine, to collect Peter who was already pacing up and down the driveway outside, waiting. He took his suitcase to the car and collected a letter from the postman which he noticed was addressed to him. He introduced himself to Matt Riordan and then turned to say Goodbye to Monique. Riordan observed that she was crying and overheard her say to Peter that she would miss him greatly. Peter thanked her for their great kindness when he needed them and said that he would keep in touch. They waved to each other as the car drove out of sight.

During the journey, Peter opened the envelope which was postmarked Dublin and he recognised the handwriting as Rosaleen's. The contents of that letter disturbed and distressed him greatly. It read as follows:

6a Burlington Mansions,
Dublin.

Friday.

Dear Peter,
I heard only the other day that you had left the priesthood some time ago. I hope that you are well, after your traumatic experience. Peter, I have something to tell you that I can't tell anyone else. I'm three months pregnant and James has walked out on me. He is not coming back and I don't want him to. I'm very frightened and don't know what to do. I'm terrified that my parents and friends will find out. Can you help me? I know you won't let me down. I have had to leave work through illness and they will dismiss me anyway when they find out. I have no phone - can you please write and come to see me please, Peter,
Rosaleen.

Peter was shocked by the news - what could he do to help her? he wondered. He would have to see her as her letter suggested how distressed she was.

When Matt and himself arrived at Kerrigart Stud, Clark Beswell was already there to welcome him. He wished him well before taking him on a lightning tour of the vast Estate. By nightfall, they still hadn't covered half of the grounds but he had met most of the employees with whom he would be associating.

Peter's apartment, situated above the stables, was well appointed; a two bedroomed flat with living room, kitchen, bathroom and toilet, well furnished and nicely decorated. There was a typed form on the living room table which outlined his duties and details of his employment. He was to be paid £750 per annum and had the rent free flat thrown in, while he remained in the employ of the Beswell family. Peter was very impressed - he could now, he felt sure, be able to save some money weekly and gradually get on his feet. At last he was independent. After going to bed, he thought of Rosaleen's plight and how he might be able to help her. It was midnight and he fell asleep, totally exhausted.

The following morning he was awakened by the sound of Matt's voice calling him from the yard below. Matt had been delegated to show him around for the first few days until he familiarised himself with his daily routine. "Mornin' Peter - are you up?....we rise early around here, you know." Peter opened the window and thanked him for the call. Within the space of a few minutes he was washed and dressed and running down the stairs and out into the yard where Matt was sitting in the truck. "I bet you're not used to getting up this early," Matt said to him. "You'll find it strange for the first week or so until you settle in." "I'm a farmer's son you know Matt - and at college we were up earlier than this every morning." "My missus has the breakfast ready for us - we'll go down there first," said Matt. "I suppose you know how to drive? Don't worry about the licence - it will be only around the estate for the moment." Peter admitted that he had not learned but would appreciate a few lessons. "You looked very worried after reading that letter on the journey here yesterday - is there anything wrong?" "Ah nothing - just a friend of mine in trouble - that's all....I'm worried about her." "I hope you haven't put her in the family way," said Matt, jokingly. "I have not, but someone else has," said Peter angrily, "and he's gone off and left her."

They pulled up outside Matt's house and went in, where his wife had already prepared the breakfast for both of them. "This is Mai," said Matt....

Matt Riordan was a local man around forty years of age who had worked with Beswells since leaving primary school and worked his way up to Estate Manager from stable lad. Peter's first impressions of Matt and his wife Mai were very favourable. Mai was a homely type of woman, small and quite plump, with a very good sense of humour. "Nice to meet you," said Mai, wiping her right hand in her apron before shaking his hand. "I hope you will be very happy here - pull in there to the table and get that down you - you'll need it before the day is over - won't he Matt?" Matt nodded in agreement and they both tucked into a fine hearty breakfast of bacon, eggs, sausages and black pudding. "Are you able to cook, Peter?" enquired Mai...."Matt will show you the village store where you can get anything you require. You will have to find yourself a nice girl now to look after you but a fine-looking fellow like you will have no bother," she laughed, as she poured a second mug of tea for him. "You're always welcome to drop in anytime," said Mai...."we have two school-going girls....they'd be delighted for a bit of help with the homework."

After breakfast, Peter was driven to the stables and introduced to the employees who were just turning up for their day's work. Matt Riordan's house was owned by the Beswells and rented to him at one shilling per week nominal rent. It was known as the

Lodge.

Within weeks, Peter was becoming quite competent behind the wheel of the Ford truck which was at his disposal for his daily routine, as it was his intention to get a driving licence soon so that he could make the occasional journey outside the Beswell Estate. At that time in Ireland, there was no driving test....all that was required was the appropriate fee, a few personal details and a nod from a Policeman.

# Chapter 14

Peter was riding in from a canter on one of the horses when he noticed a car parked in front of his apartment. It was Catherine Beswell, sitting in the driving seat waiting for him to arrive. "Hi, Peter," she shouted. "You have settled in well - how are you enjoying it so far?" she enquired. "Oh, very well Catherine, thanks - and how are you? Matt and his wife Mai are very good to me, and guess what Catherine, I'm learning to cook." "Good stuff," she answered. "I have some provisions in the boot of the car which you will need. Let's take it in, shall we?" Peter stabled the horse, took the boxes from the car and brought them upstairs. Catherine followed him, carrying a bottle of something that looked like sherry to Peter. "We must have a little party - just the two of us - this is very special wine from the French Medoc Region," she said, "and it will do nicely for your little house-warming party." "This is a surprise," said Peter, "but I have no glasses." "Don't fret, I think of everything," she answered. "They're in the car - take the keys and fetch them, please." Catherine was dressed in a tight-fitting pair of slacks and a revealing sweater - which left nothing to Peter's imagination. "I must have a quick wash and shave," Peter said, when he returned with the glasses. "Hurry now - while I pour the drinks." She paced up and down the living room as she sipped her glass of wine, calling out to Peter to get a move on as she was a very impatient woman. Finally, Peter entered from the bathroom wearing a T-shirt and trousers and took his glass of wine. "Cheers - and good luck," she said, while touching his glass "and here's to many get-togethers." Peter was lost for words and didn't reply when she took the glass of wine from his hand, left both on the table and put her arms around his neck. "Let's dance Peter - we have no music - I'll hum a little piece instead," she said, as they moved gracefully around the living room floor. She danced very close to him and smelt of that beautiful fragrance he had experienced the night at her party. He pulled away from her, picked up his glass and gulped it back. "Peter," she said, "you should sip this delicious wine. Darling, let me pour you another." They sat next to each other on the sofa when she suddenly said to him "Peter - I have something to ask you and it's very personal but you must tell me truthfully." "What is it?", asked Peter, looking startled. "Have you ever been to bed with a girl?", she enquired, as she looked him straight in the eyes. Peter was flabbergasted at this line of questioning and said - "I've had a girlfriend but we didn't do that," he stammered. "I know your background darling," said Catherine, "and this is why I ask you - you see I know you have been studying for the priesthood and they don't allow such things - or do they?" she enquired. "Everything we say or do, Peter, is an absolute secret on my part and I hope on yours as well," she went on. She put her arms around him and kissed him - his glass of wine spilling over his trousers. "Never mind," she purred - "let's forget the drinks for the moment - kiss me darling." Peter by now was excited by her and obeyed. They kissed passionately and began to caress each other in a way that developed into a frenzy for both of them until they were on the floor. He felt her body writhing as she pushed herself against him, ripping off her sweater in sudden tugs with her right hand. Peter found her luscious breasts and kissed and sucked them in an overwhelming frenzy of passion as he wrestled to undo his own clothing. He knelt beside her, pulling off her slacks to reveal black underwear the sight of which drove him wild. "I want you darling," she

64

pleaded with him. "I've wanted you since I first laid eyes on you - tell me, did you want me when you met me?", she whispered, and then kissed his body all over. "I'm going to teach you to love me," she said passionately, as she started with the insides of his thighs. He was going wild for her as he finally thrust himself into her and loved her with a passion that he didn't think himself capable of. "Where did you learn to love?" she constantly repeated - "It was Monique, wasn't it? - tell me, tell me, tell me," she kept asking. Peter said nothing but held her close to him, kissing her gently on her forehead and face. "Monique would be very jealous if she knew this, Peter - she must never know - she is in love with you - do you know that?" she enquired. Peter sat up and looked at her. "How could you say that, Catherine? Monique is my cousin's wife you know." "I am not a fool, Peter. Call it woman's intuition if you like - she never said so - but I know. Have you been to bed with her? Come on - tell me please - I have to know," she enquired sternly. Peter did not reply but whispered into her ear that he wanted her again -

Catherine left at midnight but not before Peter pleaded with her that nobody must know about this - and least of all - her husband, Clark, or indeed Monique. "Don't worry yourself about my husband," she said. "Worry," said Peter, "what about my job - or my life if he found out?" Catherine laughed at his concern - "I'm concerned too," she replied, "but it is that Monique will be invited here - has she been here yet?" she enquired. Peter said that Monique was his good friend, and no more. "Does that satisfy you?" "Yes you did," she laughed, as she put on her clothes and walked towards the door. "Peter - when I come to see you again - I have something very important to tell you - do you want me to come to see you soon?" she

65

enquired. "Of course," said Peter, as they kissed each other goodnight. "I bet some of the staff will see that you have been here," Peter observed. "So what - isn't this my property! I can come and go as I like," she replied. She raced down the stairs and banged the ground floor main door as she jumped into her car and sped off into the night. Peter was totally confused that she suddenly had such a hold on him. He wanted her with a wicked passion but also knew that it was a highly dangerous liaison.

# Chapter 15

On the morning after Catherine's visit to Peter's apartment, he was still pondering his involvement with her, when he saw the postman approaching the front door. It was a letter which had been re-directed to him from Jerome's house. The handwriting was familiar although she had written to him only twice before, when he was a Clerical Student at "Broadlands" Novitiate. It was from his sister, Mary Kate. As he opened it, thoughts ran through his mind that he should have written to tell her of his new job and rent free apartment. Inside the envelope, he found two letters - one of them sealed. He read Mary Kate's letter -

> *Mountain View,*
> *Kilrane,*
> *Killavone.*

> *Monday 14th,*

*Dear Peter,*

*You should by now have heard from poor Rosaleen in Dublin who is in some kind of trouble which she did not tell me about. She has asked me to contact you without delay in case you didn't get her letter. The other letter enclosed is from her to you and is marked 'Personal'. We must help her if we can. Can you telephone me at Killavone Post Office on Thursday at 4 pm where I will be waiting for your call as it seems*

*urgent that we do something for her.*
                              *Your loving sister,*
                                *Mary Kate.*


Peter opened the second letter addressed to him and read its contents.

                              *6a Burlington Mansions,*
                                        *Dublin.*
                                  *Saturday 12th.*


*Dear Peter,*


*Did you get my letter which I sent to you at Jerome's house? Are you still there? Please help me, Peter - I know you will - in case you haven't received my other letter, I am nearly four months pregnant. You have met the scoundrel who did it - it was James whom I took to see you that time at "Broadlands". He has now gone back to England and has made no contact whatsoever since he left. Peter, I am helpless to look after the mess I have gotten myself into. I have borrowed some money from a friend I knew at work, which has kept me going, but I want your advice. Maybe we should tell Mary Kate. I am watching the Postman every day for your reply. I know you won't let me down.*
                              *Fond regards.*
                                *Rosaleen.*


Peter re-read the letter several times and went to his apartment to think it over. He had to do something quickly for her. He went down to the stable and saddled up one of the horses and galloped across the Estate to Matt Riordan's house. When he appeared at the open front door, Matt was just leaving the breakfast table. "You timed that one well, Peter - the teapot is still hot." Mai came out of the bedroom where she was preparing her two little girls for school and greeted him warmly. "You're out early, Peter, what state of hunger are you in?" "I had a cup of tea earlier on - but I would be grateful for a quick bite to eat," he said. "Pull in there to the table - I'll put on a couple of rashers of bacon and perhaps some fried bread?" "That will be just fine - thank you Mai." As he settled in to the table, he told them that a friend of his was in a spot of bother. "I knew it all along - it's that girl you got the letter from - you were reading it the morning I delivered you to the apartment," said Matt. "That's right," said Peter, "I have come this morning to ask for help. I regard you as my friends. I don't know how to ask you - how can I say?" "She's expecting, isn't she?" said Mai as if to help him explain. "Yes, she is - I'll tell you the full story - and you must understand it wasn't me who was responsible."

Matt and Mai listened intently as she poured herself a large mug of strong tea, nodding encouragingly every time Peter faltered. When he had finished, Mai was most sympathetic, and recounted instances for him where young girls of her own acquaintance had babies out of wedlock, only to be denounced from the pulpits of their churches. "Mai is right," said Matt, "and they're not a hundred miles from here either - Christianity how are you!" "Matt's sister is a nun with the Order of the Nativity in Dublin - a grand wee girl who understands the ways of the world - I'll get in touch with her before the day is out," said Mai. "I know she will do everything she can to help the little girl.'' Peter couldn't believe his luck that he had decided to come and tell both of them about Rosaleen's plight. He promptly gave Mai Rosaleen's address to pass on to Sr. Bridget in the Convent and thanked them both for their help, kindness and generosity.

Mary Kate was waiting by the telephone at Killavone Post Office on Thursday at seven minutes past four o'clock when the call finally came through to the Postmaster. ''Is that you, Peter?'' asked the voice at the other end of the line. ''We have a very bad line - can you hear me?'' ''This is me,'' said Peter, ''I have some good news regarding Rosaleen's letter but I can't tell you on this telephone. I'll have to see you in person - can we arrange that?'' He was only too aware that there could be other ears glued to the extension phone, trawling for any snippets of information that would come along the line. ''Can you come down to Wexford? I'll meet you at the station,'' he told her. ''I'll be there,'' said Mary Kate, and bade him goodbye.

Matt and Mai Riordan with Peter, met Mary Kate from the Limerick train on the Saturday and brought her to their home where they told her the full story. She was overjoyed to hear that Sr. Bridget had already made contact with Rosaleen and arrangements were in hand to look after her in the critical months leading up to the birth of her baby.

Mai and Mary Kate joined the Dublin train on Sunday morning, a trip which was to be an experience for both of them - neither had been in the big city before.

# Chapter 16

With the women gone to Dublin to visit Rosaleen and a baby sitter obtained for the two children, Matt Riordan felt that it was an opportune time to have a 'man to man' chat, as he called it, with Peter. He decided to take him for a few drinks to his local pub 'The Drunken Piper'. Matt called for drinks at the bar and settled across the way at a table near the fire. He asked for two bottles of stout and two half ones. "Bring them over to the table like a good man," he said to the barman. "I won't beat about the bush, Peter - there's a few things I want to discuss with you and a number of details you should know about." "Fire away," said Peter. "Well, we have a good understanding of one another and you have taken us into your confidence - I would like to do likewise now - I heard you had a visit from Mrs. Beswell the other night. I even know what time she left and I didn't see the woman at all. This is an awful place for gossip, Peter. You'll have to be careful what you do around here - particularly when it is the boss's wife." "Hold on a minute," said Peter. "Yes, Catherine did call the other night but surely that's no crime, is it?" Matt shrugged his shoulders. "Look lad, it's none of my business - I'm just putting you right about one or two things - you wouldn't want people talking about you before you are warm in the place. So you're on first name terms with her - I've never called her anything but Mrs. Beswell all the time I've known the woman, and I wouldn't dream of it," said Matt. Peter studied him before he replied, "You see, Matt, I know them both quite well through my cousin, Jerome and his wife -" "Oh, by the way - Mrs Dunley called to see you when you had gone to Wexford - she left this letter for you and wanted to

71

know where your apartment was," said Matt. Peter stuffed the letter in his pocket to open it later. "You don't know much about the Beswells - so I can let you know things you should know about and anything I tell you is in strict confidence - is that clear?" Peter pulled closer to Matt, and said, "I'm all ears." "For a start," said Matt, "you'll never meet the likes of her for men - young and old, married and single." "Oh, come now," Peter interrupted him, "she can't be as bad as she's painted," he continued with a hint of annoyance "I know the woman - she seems above board to me." "Look - do you want to know the truth or not?", growled Matt. "Because if you will let me tell you -" "O.K.," Peter interrupted. "Clark Beswell, our boss is a homosexual - is that what you call them fellows? A queer, the lads around here call him. I don't know much about them." "I met one or two in College - I suppose God made them too," said Peter. Matt continued "There was a young man who had your job recently - Derek something or other - yes, Derek Kent they called him. I hadn't much to do with him. He didn't last long however - they used to say that Clark and he were lovers if you can picture that," said Matt, lighting another Woodbine cigarette from the fire. Matt always bought a small pack of Woodbines when he went to the pub but never smoked otherwise. "Derek Kent," said Peter, thoughtfully, "there is a mound of letters up at my flat addressed to him." "There they'll stay now - I think he went back to Canada after he fell out with Mrs. Beswell. She went up there one night and caught Clark and he together - there was absolute bedlam - he left soon after. Don't get me wrong, Peter, - she's a lovely looking woman - and she has put up with a lot. He married her for show only. They have been married more than ten years and there is no family there." Peter now wished to find out as much as he could about Catherine. "And who are the other men she is supposed to knock around with?" he enquired. Matt looked away before answering that one. "Would it surprise you to know that your own cousin is at the top of the queue - he has been seen here and there with her recently. They say that his missus has a lot to put up with also." Peter was reminded of the letter in his pocket from Monique but didn't open it. He also remembered the way Jerome and Catherine had kissed that night when they arrived at Beswell's party. It was a fruitful night's information, he thought as they drove back to the Estate, Matt dropping him off at the flat. As the truck swung around, the headlights picked out a car parked outside the stables, with a lady sitting at the wheel. Matt stared at Peter as he bade him goodnight and sped away.

Peter recognised the car as Monique's and walked over to her. She opened the door and said "Hello, stranger - why didn't you come over to see me since?" "What a surprise to see you! Come on in and see my new apartment - I have your letter in my pocket but haven't had a chance to read it - I just collected it from the man who drove me home. I've been so busy settling in - but I would have contacted you this week now that I have found my feet so to speak," said Peter. They walked upstairs and into the flat. Monique sat in the comfortable chair by the fire side.

Peter sat opposite and invited her to have a drink. "Would you like a glass of wine?" he enquired. "I have a delicious variety from the Medoc Region of France." "How co-incidental," snapped Monique when she saw the bottle. "That is Catherine's favourite tipple - it is very hard to come by, but I know that she got a case of it recently - from Jerome, in fact, when he returned from France." Peter didn't know where to look, he was so embarrassed - "that's right, she sent me over a bottle when I got here." "You mean she delivered a bottle in person, liar," she fumed. Peter changed the subject and told her how well she looked. "Anyway, Peter, I didn't call to talk about Catherine - but to tell you something that concerns both of us. "What is that?" he enquired. "Peter, I have missed two periods - in other words, I am pregnant with your baby." Peter collapsed on the settee. "What are you saying, Monique?" "I am expecting a baby - that's what I am saying," she repeated slowly and deliberately. "Well, that's great news for both of you," said Peter, recovering from the initial shock. "I suppose Jerome is pleased." "I don't think you heard me correctly - it is your baby. Jerome doesn't know - he hasn't been home to tell him." She caught Peter's hand and held it in hers - gazing at him. "Oh no - not another baby - what am I going to do?" said Peter. "What are you talking about? What do you mean, another baby?" she enquired. "Have you made someone else pregnant?" Peter composed himself and said quietly, "Sorry, Monique, the other baby expected is with a friend of mine in Dublin. She is an ex-girlfriend." Monique was horrified. "I thought you were going to be a priest before you came to us." "No, you don't understand - the baby is not mine - I'm just trying to help her," he explained.

There was absolute silence between them for a few moments until Peter blurted out - "What are we going to do? Jerome will go crazy - he'll kill me when he finds out - How do you know it's me?" "I know it's you," she answered, "but Jerome will never find out. It's his baby for all he will know. He always wanted a baby - now he's going to be a father. It's our secret, Peter - for always." He pondered what she said for a while before asking, "What about the timing?" "Do you mean, were he and I together - well the answer is yes - around the same time

74

you made me pregnant. I conceived that very first night with you." Peter did not know what to say or do, he was so confused and frightened. She got up to leave and asked him to promise to see her soon and that he would not see Catherine. He promised her that he would call to see her at her house soon, kissed her gently on the cheek and escorted her to her car. He knew in his heart and soul that, whatever the promise of calling to see her, he couldn't keep the one about not seeing Catherine - in fact, he desired Catherine now more than ever.

# Chapter 17

Back in Kilrane, in the Parish of Killavone, the neighbours tongues were wagging furiously - for it was a story that they could get their teeth into - Nora Dunley was getting married again; this time the new man in her life was Bertie Flanagan, a hackney cab owner who had recently come to live in the area, from another county. It had become the topic of conversation in the village that John Dunley was hardly cold in his grave than his widow had a new interest. Hadn't he been seen visiting the Dunley home quite often? - a man that had never put his foot over the threshold when John Dunley was alive. The more charitable neighbours said it was only friendship between Nora and Bertie Flanagan, a widower in his early fifties. How could she even contemplate it? they thought, sure he wasn't even her type, and knew nothing about farming which was even worse. Bertie had met Nora several times when she had hired him to go to town to attend to the various business commitments she had, since John passed away. Her son, Joe, had also used him occasionally since he inherited Aunt Annie's house and farm and his solicitor had called him in with Annie when the signing over took place. Joe and Bertie got on well together and were card-playing partners whenever there was a game locally. What fuelled the gossip in recent weeks was Nora's visit to town with Bertie when they were seen having tea together after coming out of her solicitor's office. Rumours were rife that things were serious between them because - why were they visiting the solicitor together, neighbours asked, if they weren't thinking of tying the knot? Langan, the blacksmith, said that the gossip about them was on everyone's tongue - he had good reason to know, given the wide cross-section of the farming community who visited him to have their horses shod. "What did Flanagan know about farming?" was the common question on all their lips "and what did she see in him anyway? - sure he wasn't half the man that John Dunley was - God rest him."

It wasn't long before the story came to a head, when one morning as Nora was collecting some provisions from the village , a curious old lady brushed against her, excused herself and said "How long is it until your husband's anniversary Nora? I suppose you'll wait until after that to give us the big day out?" Nora turned quickly around from the counter where she was paying for her groceries and in a furious voice said "I beg your pardon - I don't seem to know you - repeat that please." The old lady picked up her shopping bag and as she was going out the door turned back and said, "Let the dead rest in peace for another while." Nora, visibly shaken, turned to Mrs. O'Gorman the shopkeeper and asked her what she made of it. "Well Nora," she said, "I'd be telling a lie if I said I didn't know what she meant. There is a lot of gossip around the place about Mr. Flanagan and yourself - you know what the people are like - don't take any notice of them, love." "I will get to the bottom of this no matter how long it takes me," said Nora as she thanked the shopkeeper for the information and made her way briskly down the street in the direction of Canon Jim Mulraney's house. He was just leaving as she came up the path towards him. "Good day, Nora - what a pleasant surprise to see you," he said. "Come right in." "How are you, Canon?" she asked. "I won't be delaying you but there is something I have to discuss." "Sit yourself down there, Nora," he said, pulling up a chair for her. "I am very distressed at something I heard in the village while shopping this morning," Nora said, as she fought back the tears. "Don't be upset - carry on and if I can be of any help -" "Well," she continued, "they are gossiping about me and Bertie Flanagan who I am friendly with." "Who is Bertie Flanagan?" he enquired - "is he the hackney man who lives over the road?" "Yes, he is," continued Nora, "and I am very hurt about what they are saying about John Dunley not yet being cold in his grave. The truth is, Father, that I am very friendly with Bertie and we have discussed settling down together but that is surely our business only, don't you agree, Canon?" "I do and I don't - if you know what I mean - what I'm saying is - you mustn't entertain him in your house until after you are married - otherwise the people will be talking about you." Nora rose from the chair and said "That is precisely why I'm here to see you - to stop the gossip." She went to leave the house, thinking that her visit wasn't that worthwhile when he stopped her at the door and said "Be at the eleven o'clock Mass on Sunday next and ask Bertie to be there too but don't be there together - do you understand?"

She went home to Kilrane wondering what lay in store on Sunday and called at Bertie's house on the way out to let him know what had transpired. "Sit in," said Bertie, "I'll give you a lift home - that'll keep the tongues wagging for another while."

On Sunday morning, the church was packed as usual for the eleven o'clock Mass. The Canon always said that particular one and he was assured of a full house because of the brevity of his sermons. He was known far and wide in the parish as the priest who kept them the shortest time on Sunday. However, this Sunday was to be an exception, they soon realised, as Canon Jim ascended the pulpit and blessed himself with the sign of the cross...."My dear people," he started, "to-day I am going to talk to you about the Commandments of God and the particular one I have chosen - I am sure you can all quote with me from your catechisms - is 'Thou shalt not bear false witness against thy neighbour'. How many of us assembled here today in the house of God realise when we recite these words how often we break this commandment of God?...by speaking ill of our neighbours...by bearing false messages about our neighbours...rotten unfounded lies about them...How often do we realise the mortal sin we commit by bearing this false witness?...my dear people I ask you to examine your consciences...and each one of us ask ourselves, have we told lies about any of our neighbours...or have we listened to gossip and added to it, turning the truth into a travesty. I say to all of you here and now...when you go forth from this congregation, restore the good name of the person you have maligned, whether it be idle gossip in the shops or the pubs or in your place of work.''

Suddenly, the silence was broken as a slight murmur seemed to creep through the church. It was widely known at this stage, that the originator of the gossip about Nora and Bertie was none other than Nora's workman, called Jimmy, who had been spreading the rumours in the local pubs after he had taken a bottle of stout too many. No one knew his surname, he had come many years ago to Dunley's farm as a workman and had stayed, making a little home for himself in an outhouse at the back of the Dunley homestead. Since John had died, Nora had noticed that Jimmy had asserted himself greatly and maybe he now felt that he would be a likely suitor for her. After all, he felt that he knew the running of the place and he was roughly her own age, give or take a year or two. After Canon Jim's sermon, people began to point the finger at Jimmy, and Nora was warned to be careful about the way she dealt with him. Her suspicions were finally aroused when Bertie's car tyres were deflated during a visit to her home and she informed the Gardai. He got off with a warning but it did not deter him from mischief making at every opportunity.

# Chapter 18

For the first time in his life, Peter was receiving regular pay packets and he felt that he was getting on well in his employment. He loved the job with the country's finest horses and had a dedicated staff of stable lads, boys and girls between the ages of sixteen and nineteen years old.

He wondered what Matt Riordan was thinking when he saw Monique parked outside the flat on their return from the pub - only this time it was the cousin's wife and not the boss's wife as Matt had referred to Catherine. His telephone was now installed and would be operational later that day. He knew that he would now be able to call the telephone exchange to put him through to his various friends - he also wondered would Catherine telephone him or should he himself telephone her and thank her for having it installed. He decided what a good idea that was and what a marvellous opportunity to talk with her again. He also wanted her advice about various items of clothing that he needed, particularly a good double-breasted suit which he liked. He remembered the way James was attired that day when Rosaleen brought him along to "Broadlands" to meet him. That was all he admired about him though, after what he had done to Rosaleen and then left her to face the consequences alone. Monique suddenly cropped into his mind and what she had told him about being pregnant with his child. A cold shiver ran through him - after all, he now thought, why should he himself be so critical of James, when he had made his cousin's wife pregnant? Wasn't that far worse? he pondered. But Monique WANTED a baby and couldn't have one by Jerome; she was now very happy to be expecting and to have a Dunley for a father, even if it wasn't her husband. He felt that she loved him, but why had he to meet Catherine who was now the subject of his total obsession? He compared them both in his mind and Catherine always scored the higher.

That evening he picked up his new telephone and heard it ring in the Exchange. When the operator answered, he asked for Clark Beswell's home number and was immediately connected. "Good evening - Clark Beswell here, can I help you?" Peter was taken aback momentarily as he had expected Catherine to answer. "Hello, Clark - this is Peter Dunley - I just rang to say thank you for having the telephone installed. Naturally I'm thrilled with it - this is the very first call from it." Clark replied, "How have you settled in? I haven't had a chance to keep in touch because of travel commitments and a busy work schedule - I hope my wife Catherine has been looking after you?" Peter nervously replied that she had been very good to him and had let him know that the telephone would be installed. "Good - now Peter, I am in a particularly buoyant mood this evening - absolutely great news for Kerrigart Stud - we've swung the big one, the biggest deal of the century - with the French and the Arabs - the Egyptians to be exact...this is what we have been waiting for...I have just returned from Cairo where I met their Minister for Trade - both Governments have been involved naturally...In fact our own Minister will travel out with me on my next visit there. It is a deal of national importance involving the export of our very best thoroughbreds. It is great news for all of us Peter and more responsibility for you ultimately," said Clark enthusiastically. Peter couldn't believe his luck that he had telephoned at such an opportune time. "By the way, Peter, Catherine wants a word with you." Catherine then took the telephone - after bidding Clark goodbye as he rushed off to a meeting. "Lovely to hear your golden voice - and talking about voices, I am inviting you to join a new show which I am producing later this year," she said. "It is 'OKLAHOMA' - do you know anything from it?" "Can't say I do, but thank you for thinking of me." "I'm always thinking of you, Peter darling," she answered. "What did you think of that fantastic news from Clark? It truly means that Kerrigart is now firmly on the international map...the demand for our bloodstock is going to be huge." Catherine could hardly contain herself with the excitement of it all. "I'm so happy darling," she said to Peter "and how about you?" "Me? I'm very happy too...I want to say how delighted I am for you..." "What do you mean, 'for you'----for us, Peter...you are part of it too." "Of course, Catherine," he replied, "I'm over the moon about it all." "Now darling, we must meet really soon because as I've already said, I have much to discuss with you. Be in your apartment tonight. I shall drive over to see you later." "I'll be expecting you," said Peter, before they hung up.

No sooner had he replaced his telephone than Peter dialled the Exchange again and asked to be put through to Monique Dunley. He felt that this was the best course of action in case she called his apartment unannounced and found Catherine there. Monique was overjoyed to hear him at the other end of the line. "I thought I would ring you - you see I'm playing with my new toy -" Monique interrupted him, "When did you have the phone installed?" "It was a complete surprise," said Peter, "the telephone man arrived at the beginning of the week and installed it. I have just put the phone down from talking to Clark - did you hear their fantastic news about the export deal with Egypt?" "So I heard from Jerome...he was with Clark on the journey from London...they are celebrating in style tonight at the Club with Clark's fellow directors---no place there for women I was informed...strictly a stag night." The moment she mentioned Jerome's name, thoughts of the pregnancy surfaced. "Did you tell him...I mean did you tell Jerome about the baby?", he enquired nervously. "Yes I did of course - it was the first news I greeted him with - he is over the moon about everything - he even joked that it must have been all the excitement when you were around here. "What did you reply?", asked Peter cautiously. "What do you think I told him, for God's sake? 'You're going to be a daddy, Jerome' I said. He looked at me incredulously for a moment and then shouted 'Brilliant - absolutely brilliant - I remember the night it happened darling - do you?' 'Of course I do - I shall never forget it - do you want a boy or a girl?'-", Peter suddenly interrupted, - "So everything is O.K. then - I mean...he will never suspect, will he?" "Unless I tell him of course," she teased. "You know, Monique, there is always the possibility that it was him rather than me." "Oh, come off it, for Christ's sake - we've been trying for the past ten years without success and then you come along - you're not a complete fool - look, don't get a coronary about it - when the baby arrives it will be Jerome's...O.K.? - but you will be my lover...I hate to make it sound like a deal Peter." He looked aghast at the inference and felt that it was a form of blackmail but this wasn't the time to be splitting hairs - he was delighted that Jerome would never know that his cousin had been in bed with his wife...especially as he had treated him so well when he fled the priestly Novitiate. He was also learning fast, of the wiles of women when they really wanted something. He suddenly remembered that the telephone was linked to the Exchange. "What if anyone has been eavesdropping on this conversation?", he reminded her. "That's the chance you take," she said, using a deliberate pun which was not wasted on Peter as he said goodbye. He felt that he had to spend some time with her soon.

# Chapter 19

Catherine was ringing the ground floor doorbell to his apartment, as Peter looked out the bedroom window, having heard the sound of a motor car in the courtyard. "Let yourself in - the key is in the lock," he shouted down. Catherine raced up the stairs and into the living room where he threw his arms around her in a vice-like grip....the long embrace turned into gentle kissing and from that to long, hungry, passionate kissing and caressing....there was no word spoken between them....they hungered for each other so much....They stumbled backwards towards his bedroom as he dropped to his knees and kissed her body all over....He complimented her on the fabulous blue dress she was wearing....the scent of her perfume drove him wild. "I bought it for you," she whispered...."I want you Catherine - I desperately want you now," he moaned...."Come on darling - let's not waste time - let's get into bed," she said, as they both undressed each other in a frenzy of excitement and passion....they lay on the bed and he continued kissing her all over until they finally made love....as they loved, he could hear the front door banging in the wind - Catherine had not secured it when she entered, but this was not the moment to be concerned about such mundane matters, even though anyone could walk in and catch them in the act....the danger of their liaison seemed to excite him more and more. Finally, as he lay, spent, beside her, he asked her if she knew that the main door was open and Clark, Monique, or even Matt Riordan could walk in and catch them...."Oh - just forget everybody," she exclaimed "and love me like you've just done - you must tell me something here and now, Peter; who was the first girl you went to bed with?" Peter answered quickly, "You, dearest Catherine - there hasn't been anyone else." "I said I want the absolute truth Peter - please answer me - you are going to tell me, aren't you darling?" She looked into his eyes before kissing him again. Peter finally dropped his guard and said quickly that Monique was the first and only woman he had slept with before her. He had hardly uttered the name Monique when Catherine suddenly sat up in bed and made attempts to find her underclothing when Peter said "I'm only joking - honest." "You're not joking Peter, damn you, I knew it....I knew it....How many times did it happen?" Peter tried to stop her talking by attempting to kiss her where she liked being kissed most....and before long he was loving her again....this time with a furious passion. "You are a wonderful lover," she kept repeating. "I love you crazily Peter darling -" "I love you too Catherine - more than anything in the world - don't let anyone else ever do this to you - ever - do you hear me? Please promise me...." She stayed silent while he went on...."you have had many lovers, Catherine - why should I believe that you love me now?" She finally spoke "I do love you darling and some day I'll prove it to you - I'm nearly twenty years older than you," she cried, "and I hate to think of it. Does it matter to you?" "Not in the slightest," Peter assured her, "you are the most beautiful woman in the world."

When they had dressed, he poured her a cup of coffee and they sat down together. "I have a lot to tell you," she whispered. She sipped from the cup as she told him:. "It is widely known that Clark and I lead separate lives - under the same roof, so to speak - he never touches me nowadays." "I never want him to either," interrupted Peter. "You see, Peter, he is a homosexual - he used to be bi sexual - that is, if you don't know, with a desire for both sexes - nowadays, it is males only with him."

90

Peter knew well what she was talking about - he had lectures on the subject in the Seminary at "Broadlands", an era in his life that had, by now, become a memory. He had also been briefed by Matt Riordan about Clark, but he would never let him down by repeating what he had told him. "I am quite shocked - but in a way, I am also pleased, Catherine." "Why is that, darling?", she asked. "Because I want you to be mine always....Now tell me about your boyfriends please." "O.K. darling I'll tell you....for a start I have been seeing your cousin Jerome on and off for some time....now that'll shock you, won't it?" "Oh my God!", said Peter, - "and who knows about this?" "I don't know and I don't care, because it's over now," she assured him. She then asked him how much he really knew about Jerome. "Not a lot to be honest with you - I know he is wealthy but I haven't a clue about his business interests." "O.K., I will tell you what I know," said Catherine. "Jerome fell on his feet by marrying Monique - it is she who has made him what he is today. It was her money - Clark is a director of two of his companies. He approached him with a partnership idea and Clark accepted." "And you accepted when Jerome asked you out," Peter said angrily. "You are getting possessive darling, aren't you?" she said jokingly. "I like my men to be possessive." "Please change that word to the singular from now on," protested Peter.

It was time for her to leave as it was well past midnight. After kissing good-night, he promised that he would telephone tomorrow - he wanted her to go shopping with him; he told her he valued her judgment in the clothing he would wear from now on.

# Chapter 20

Peter's friend, Paddy Morrissey, was now a Deacon of the Church and would, with God's help, be ordained a priest in nine months' time. Peter learned this in a letter he received from his old friend, a letter posted from "Broadlands" Seminary. From the tenor of the letter, it was obvious that he had written to him on a number of previous occasions although they had not been received by Peter. The letter read as follows:

> *"Broadlands" Ecclesiastical Seminary,*
> *Co. Louth.*
> *14th October.*
>
> *Dear Peter,*
>
> *While I am surprised that you have not answered my previous letters, I am more than disappointed that you didn't think of contacting me since your departure from here. I understand perfectly well that you would have wished to have made a final break with the College, but I found it hard to take, that you totally renounced your friendship with me. We went back a long way, Peter - too far back to have forgotten. I remember distinctly, for example, the hospitality extended to me at your home at Killavone, when you first met Rosaleen, and your excitement, having returned from the dance that you had a date with her. I was part of the plot hatched out with your brother Joe to get you to see her on that dark winter evening. Her picture is still in my room here at "Broadlands". I*

*was amazed that you didn't take it with you when you
made the final break with the Seminary. I suppose she
is married by now, judging by her enthusiasm for that
fellow she brought along to meet you - I could never
forget how that visit affected you. I knew then, Peter,
that you wouldn't stick it here. It has been tough for
me too, believe me, but being a glutton for punish-
ment, I have persisted with it. I am called 'Reverend'
now and wear the dog collar - you will be required to
'salute' me in the street when you meet me.*

*Please note that you are at the top of my invitation
list for my ordination ceremony next June and I am
giving you timely notice so that you can make the
necessary arrangements. I have been in touch with
your mother who told me of your father's death, God
rest him. I was pleased to hear that she has met someone else who appears to be a nice fellow. She told me
that she would be privileged if I could assist at her re-
marriage ceremony when it takes place. Please write
to me soon and furnish me with Rosaleen's address so
that I can drop her a line about my ordination. I can
also tell her that I carry her picture around in my
breviary! I trust that Mary Kate keeps in touch. Please
Lord that this letter gets to you.*

*Kindest regards,*
*Your old friend,*
*(Rev) Paddy!*

Peter enjoyed the letter enormously from his old friend and it
brought back many memories of their schooldays together -
some pleasant, more of them horrific. He felt that it was churlish

of him not to have made contact with him before now but he felt from the letter that he was forgiven for his thoughtlessness. What a great opportunity it now offered, he thought, that Paddy would contact Rosaleen and befriend her in the trauma that she was going through. He replied immediately.

*Kerrigart Stud Farms,*
*Wexford.*
*20th October.*

*Dear Rev Father Paddy,*

*What a surprise and great thrill for me to receive your most welcome letter. All I can say is 'Forgive me, Father, for I have been guilty of the sin of omission'. My negligence is unforgivable. So much has happened to me personally since our sharing that room and many confidences together. I have entered another world, Paddy - a world of real people, wealth, beautiful women and exciting parties. The type of world I didn't know existed when I prayed with you that my vocation to the priesthood would be strengthened. I must reveal to you, however, that I haven't prayed since leaving the Seminary, except, perhaps at my father's deathbed, when I asked him to forgive me for hurting him as I obviously did when I left the priesthood. What has happened to me, you, no doubt, will find an answer for. My vocation, I now realise, was my mother's rather than mine - and I know and realise that it was far better to get out when I did rather than live a lie anymore. Maybe I'm living a lie now, Paddy, in my adopted lifestyle, but it has a strange fascination for me - whatever you might think of it. I have not one but two women, both of them married, that I have carnal knowledge of - and strange as it may seem they both need me. Yes, Reverend Paddy Morrissey, I can almost hear you say it - SINS OF THE FLESH, ADULTERY, COVETING OTHER MEN'S WIVES: they are all there - the sins we learned were the deadly ones. Is there no hope for me?*

*Please come and visit me during the holidays - you would enjoy the open spaces, the horses and maybe one or two of the parties! I enclose a separate note with Rosaleen's address. Write again soon - do please continue to keep in touch.*

*Yours,*

*Peter.*

Peter enclosed a note merely saying that Rosaleen was recovering from an illness in the Nursing Home and asked him to contact her soon. He wondered about the wisdom of his confession to his old friend - maybe, he thought, it might give him a flavour of the world outside the four walls of "Broadlands" Seminary.

# Chapter 21

Catherine collected Peter promptly as arranged for a visit to town where he was interested in selecting a wardrobe of clothing with the assistance of her experienced eye for the fashionable. They were sitting in the foyer of the Provincial Hotel sipping their morning coffee when Peter noticed a headline of the morning's newspaper. It caught his eye when a person across the way held it up. He nudged Catherine - was he reading correctly he wondered or were his eyes deceiving him? It was something about Dunley Enterprises in banner headlines. He immediately jumped to his feet and darted across to Reception where he purchased a copy. Having rushed back to Catherine, he clutched the front page and read it aloud to her. "Fraud Squad investigates Dunley Enterprises." "WHAT?", she exclaimed as she grabbed the newspaper to see for herself. She read the paragraph under the flaunting headline. "A team of fraud squad detectives are currently investigating the affairs of the Dunley Enterprises Group of Companies after discrepancies were reported to the Authorities." She broke off and looked at Peter. "It can't be," she said "- there must be some mistake." Both of them finished their coffees badly shaken as they read on. "Mr. Jerome Dunley, Chairman and Managing Director of the Group, is believed to be out of the country on business at present, but a spokesman for the company had no comment to make when reporters tried to determine the nature of the investigations." They re-ordered coffee, composed themselves as best they could and discussed what they should do. Clark Beswell was also away - so they decided they would both drive across to Monique's to bring her a copy of the newspaper, so that she could read it for herself. As they entered the driveway to her home, a posse of reporters were already gathered. Monique had been awakened by the doorbell's ringing and had opened it in her dressing gown to the two detectives who wanted to ask her some questions in Jerome's absence. She let Peter and Catherine in to the hall and told them how relieved she was to see them both. "I just don't know anything," she cried out to reporters at the front door. "Now please go away." Peter soon became the focus of the detectives attention as they were asked for their names. When Peter gave the Dunley surname they took particular interest in him until they learned that he did not work for the Dunley Organisation. They asked him, however, to keep himself available as he may be required to help them with their enquiries at a later date.

When the detectives finally left Monique's house, she tried frantically, to make contact with Jerome in London at their Associate company and was informed that they, too, were the subject of investigations in Britain. Peter and Catherine decided to take Monique with them, in view of the consternation caused by the reporters and detectives. The evening Radio bulletin carried a story that Jerome Dunley had been arrested at London's Heathrow Airport and was being escorted back to Ireland to answer serious allegations in connection with his companies. The report stated that an "alleged tangled web of deceit had been brought to light" after several months' painstaking enquiries. "What is it all about?" Monique asked them both when they arrived at Catherine's place to await details of the time of arrival of Jerome from London under escort. They telephoned the Garda Station who told them to wait until the following morning. Monique contacted her solicitor and by noon the following day, an application was accepted for Jerome's release on bail of a fifty thousand pound surety by Catherine. The alleged tangled web of deceit concerned five finance companies in the Dunley Group in association with a financial consortium in Britain involved in deals with foreign banks.

The following morning, a dishevelled Jerome Dunley and his wife Monique were driven home from the Garda Station by his solicitor while investigations continued, and they both felt that a lot of sorting out had to be done if he was to recover from this mess; 'a tangled web of deceit' that had become too complicated even for Jerome's mental agility.

A visit to his home at Killavone was long overdue, Peter thought, so many events had taken place there in recent times. There was the handing over of Aunt Annie's farm to his brother Joe who now had the responsibility of more than two hundred acres. Aunt Annie would soon be entering a Nursing Home for the Elderly. She was now in her seventies, and crippled with arthritis. Peter's mother, Nora, had a boyfriend and was seriously contemplating marriage again, this time to Bertie Flanagan, a relative newcomer to the parish. Jerome Dunley, out on bail for alleged fraud would, he knew, be the talk of the parish because of his problems, so Peter felt that both of them should travel together to visit family and friends.

Jerome collected him early for the five hour journey to Killavone. It would be a great opportunity, he anticipated, to have a long, frank discussion on the problems besetting them both. His secret that he was the father of Jerome's wife's expected child was bad enough to contemplate but now, the fraud case was looming and further enquiries were pending, according to the Gardai. Jerome barely spoke during the first leg of the journey until after they had pulled in for petrol on the way, where Jerome bought a copy of the day's paper. When he got back in the car, he scanned the headlines and found an article relating to himself - the headline read: "Dunley bailed in alleged Financial Fraud Scandal." He handed the paper to Peter as he drove off and asked him to read it aloud. "Jerome Dunley, boss of Dunley Financial Services," it said, "was arrested in London by Fraud Squad detectives investigating alleged irregularities between his group of companies and the Singland Trust of Great Britain. He was handed over to Irish Police and was bailed to appear at Wexford Court in March next. It is pointed out that Dunley Financial Services are under investigation and not Dunley Enterprises as stated earlier in the week." "At least they got some of it right this time," he snapped angrily. "When all of this is behind me I'll make those bastards hop." Peter thought it might be a good time to try out a few questions, bearing in mind that in a few hours time they would be arriving in Killavone and would be pursued by the local press as well as having to answer to the family, who were no doubt very worried about the coverage the story was getting. He soon learned that Jerome was in no mood for any further questions. Instead, he turned the tables on Peter by asking him if it was true that he was having an affair with Catherine Beswell. "I'm asking you straight out," he said. "Are you or are you not seeing her?" "Of course I'm seeing her," came the reply. "I work for the lady, don't I and indeed report to her occasionally?", said Peter. "I have seen you out together and it has to stop - do you hear me?" "If you must know, Catherine and I are fond of each other and we meet when it is convenient," Peter interrupted. "Everyone, including me, knows that you have been seeing her in the past - I know she doesn't see you any more." Jerome was fuming. "She told you - didn't she? She'll have a lot more to tell you soon when details of this mess come to light." Peter interrupted - "I know that

Clark has money invested in your companies and got a partnership for doing so." There the row ended - they were getting closer to Killavone where they would soon be with their own relatives. Peter was pleased that his relationship with Catherine had at least got an airing between both of them but he was petrified that details of his liaison with Monique would leak in Jerome's direction.

When they arrived, Jerome's first priority was to see his bedridden mother, Annie. He was sad to see how her health had deteriorated since he last saw her. He wondered if she was aware of his problems, as he parked outside the house and walked straight in to the bedroom. When they spoke, however, her main concern was that he wouldn't be annoyed that Peter's brother, Joe, had inherited the place from her. She put out her hand to greet him and said "When Joe comes in from the land, I want to talk to both of you together - you understand Jerome, why I made the decision to give him the farm? I am not able to continue now and without his help, I would not have managed - he's been good to me since I got laid up." "Of course I understand," said Jerome, kissing her on the forehead. Just then Joe entered and greeted them both. "I was just saying that Mother made the right decision when she willed you the farm in view of her health." He thought momentarily of how insignificant was the money that the farm would have fetched at auction if he had it, in comparison to the monies that exchanged hands daily in Dunley Enterprises. Aunt Annie sat up in bed and said to them both, "This land belonged to the Dunley name for as long as anyone can trace and it is only right, as Jerome said, that Joe, the man who stayed at home, should inherit it. His mother, Nora, is still a very young woman - we musn't forget that." Jerome shook Joe's hand warmly and said "I wish you the best of luck and I know you'll look after my mother as best you can." Joe nodded in agreement. Peter, meanwhile, had visited his mother's house, having arranged that his sister, Mary Kate, and brother Joe should join him there for a family get together now that Nora was seriously contemplating marriage with Bertie Flanagan. Nora went one better and said that it was a great opportunity for them to meet him.

That evening when Jerome and Peter visited the main pub in the village, they encountered Nora's workman, Jimmy, who was the worse for wear through drink and was quite obnoxious in his conversation with them, first of all about what he had gleaned from local gossip about Jerome's problems and, secondly, about Nora's intended marriage to Bertie. "I hear the Gardai have been to see you Jerome. Sure haven't they been up to see me too as if I was a criminal also," he said to them, inferring that Jerome was. "I did nothing to anyone at all, at all." He had been referring to his visit from the local Gardai after it was widely thought that he had interfered with the tyres of Bertie's car. They decided to leave the public house when the conversation turned to Nora's intended partner, who, he inferred, was marrying her "for the fine farm of land and nothing else." When they returned to Nora's house, they were introduced to Bertie Flanagan who announced that he and Nora had become engaged and would be getting married, very quietly, in the near future. Canon Jim, Nora told them, had advised Bertie and herself that it was best to do it that way, in view of the circumstances. He would soon, she told them, be publishing the banns, which gave notice of intended marriage and had to be read three times in the local church to give the opportunity of any intended objection.

# Chapter 22

The first and second reading of the banns took place without incident and it wasn't until the Canon had folded and put away the banns notice after the final reading, that a woman stood up at the back of the congregation and shouted "Bertie Flanagan has been my lawfully wedded husband for the past twenty-five years and still is. He is not allowed to marry anyone else." There was a deathly hush in the church as she continued - "This is our daughter, Monica," as she pointed to a severely retarded girl in a wheelchair next to her who appeared to be aged around twenty. Canon Jim, visibly shaken, walked slowly down the altar steps and down the long aisle to the back of the church towards them. "You are welcome, Mrs. Flanagan, to this church and you have performed a very important duty as far as church law is concerned." He gave the girl in the wheelchair a gentle pat on the head and said to the woman "This young lady is the result of your marriage union together - are there other children?" "No, Father - just her" came the reply. Canon Jim made his way to the altar to finish the Mass celebration after he had asked the lady to see him in the sacristy after the service had ended. She waited outside the door of the sacristy until he had disrobed and put away his vestments. He invited her in and pulled out a note-pad and pencil to get the details he required. She claimed that they had met in Cavan around 1930 and got married there a couple of years later. "I will have to get some matters clarified with the church records and clergy of that area, do you understand," the Canon said to her - "just formalities that have to be dealt with - but I am indeed grateful to you for coming along this morning." He warned her of the seriousness of making a false allegation and the damage and embarrassment to both partners it would be, if she was proved to be lying. When he asked her how she knew that the banns were being read in the church at the particular time, there was consternation at her reply. She was, she said, Jimmy's sister - "the Jimmy who works at Nora Dunley's." Soon afterwards the Canon went to Nora's home where he met all the family assembled for Sunday dinner and told them what the banns had revealed about Bertie. They were all shocked; it just couldn't be the case, they said. Bertie was too kind and too honest to cause this kind of hurt to Nora. The priest told them that his enquiries were not complete until he had had the Cavan church records examined. When he enquired as to where the workman Jimmy could be located, he was informed by Joe, that Sunday was his day off. "Where is the man who is the subject of these investigations?" he said, referring to Bertie Flanagan. Peter and Jerome were despatched to find him, while Joe was asked to look for Jimmy. When they arrived at Bertie's home they were informed by neighbours that Sunday was his busy day with fares in his hackney cab from the church masses. They were soon informed, however, that they had seen him take a fare from Killavone shortly after mass was over in the village. The neighbour had a description of the passengers; a tall lady and a girl in a wheelchair were assisted into the hackney cab by Bertie, together with a couple of suitcases. When the Canon heard this latest twist to the story he was very angry and consoled Nora for all the hurt the incident had provoked. "Wait until I get my hands on that scoundrel," he roared, referring to Jimmy the workman. "I'm afraid we have seen the last of him," said Joe, entering the house after he had been to the apartment that Jimmy had occupied. "He has performed his final trick - the room is empty - he is gone for good.'' Nora breathed a sigh of relief. ''Thank the Lord, and thank you Canon Jim for all your help,'' she said, as she went to the cupboard to pour him a large glass of whiskey.

# Chapter 23

While the menfolk were away, Catherine visited Monique to have dinner with her. She thought that Monique looked wretched; the combination of the dreadful trauma that Jerome's arrest had brought, coupled with her pregnancy, was taking its toll on her health. Catherine wanted to know if she had any inside information on Jerome's problems. If she knew anything she wasn't divulging it to Catherine. "He hasn't been up to form for the past few months now - even when I told him that I was expecting his baby - he didn't exactly jump for joy, even though he always wished for an heir. He has been off colour and I just can't put my finger on it." Catherine broke in, "I thought he would be overjoyed at the news of your expected child - after ten years of marriage - Monique, are you telling me the truth?" "How do you mean, Catherine?" "I'm asking you - is Jerome the father of the child you are expecting? You know there are rumours circulating that it could be Peter's?" Monique stood up and in mock horror, shouted at Catherine "I beg your pardon - do you realise what you have just said?" "I said there are rumours, Monique." "There are rumours about *you*, Catherine," she countered, "- very nasty rumours at that - very unsavoury ones too." Catherine interrupted, "Come on, let's have them then - what are you referring to - you can't make statements like that without backing them up by facts." "It's time we discussed certain things that are on my mind - to begin with - Jerome has slept with you, hasn't he? - come on, let's have it out in the open." Catherine was momentarily stunned and finally answered "I have had a drink with him - yes!" "Oh, don't give me that rubbish - you have slept with him on numerous occasions - like many others." Monique broke off to allow her to answer. Catherine was furious but stayed silent. "I can't understand this damn fascination you have for the Dunleys --- the latest gossip is that, not content with my husband, you are also having it off with Peter." Monique broke down in tears as she mentioned his name. "Monique, are you going crazy or something? He's only a child - he's only twenty-four years old." "I'm delighted you mentioned his age - you're old enough to be his mother." "Don't try to change the subject. This conversation started when I told you of the rumours circulating that Peter is the father of your expected baby," shouted Catherine. Just then the door bell rang and Monique, composing herself, walked down the hall to answer it. She could see a tall man outside through the darkened glass panel. As she opened the door the man pulled a card from his raincoat pocket and said, "Detective Inspector Keating, could I speak with Mr. Jerome Dunley, please?" "I'm afraid you can't," she replied. "He - my husband is away for a few days - can I help you?" "I'm afraid not, Madam," he said. "Could you give me the address where he can be contacted?" "Look, what is this about, Inspector? What is so urgent that you want to see him again?" "Further urgent enquiries, Mrs. Dunley - we'll find him - Good night to you." She closed the door and came down the hall sobbing into a handkerchief. "These people are like vultures," she said, as she told Catherine that it was the Gardai again looking for Jerome. Their first reaction was that they should try and contact him at Killavone - but how? They weren't even aware when he and Peter would be returning from there. Suddenly, their argument was forgotten as they both worried about what faced Jerome now.

Monique's telephone rang the following morning. It was Peter, to inform her that Jerome had been arrested in Killavone and taken into custody by the local Gardai and was now being taken back to Wexford under escort. She was mystified by the news. Peter had now to drive Jerome's car back on the return journey. The driving lessons that Matt Riordan had given him were now put to practical use on the journey home to Wexford. Later that night, Monique was informed that Jerome was being held at the Station with the possibility of being extradited to England to face serious charges there.

# Chapter 24

Rosaleen was thrilled to receive a visit from Peter's friend, Paddy, at the Convent of the Nativity where she was recuperating after her miscarriage. They had met once before when she was Peter's girlfriend, and he had seen her briefly the day she came to "Broadlands" to visit Peter with her new boyfriend, James.

Paddy arrived, dressed in his priestly attire and was the subject of much favourable attention from the nuns. He was invited to their Reception room where one of the Sisters soon arrived with a tray of tea, sandwiches and home-baked scones for Rosaleen and himself. Rosaleen entered shortly afterwards, escorted by the Reverend Mother, a rotund, red-faced woman with a very hearty laugh. When she saw him, Rosaleen burst into tears and embraced him. "Thank you, Father, for coming to see me." "Oh - you don't have to call me that yet," he laughed. When the nun made her exit, Paddy tried to make Rosaleen feel at ease with him by pulling out of his pocket, the photograph of her that Peter left behind in their room when he fled the Seminary. "I keep this in my breviary," he said to her. "I bet you didn't realise that I had a look at you as often as that," he joked. Rosaleen didn't know how to reply. "I can't believe that this is happening to me," she said, while trying to fight back the tears. He pulled a white handkerchief from his trouser pocket and wiped her cheek. "I'm crying with joy," she said finally. Paddy told her that he knew what had happened and that she must now put it behind her. "You are the sister I never had," he told her. "You have been through your hell and I wish I had known earlier of your plight but I have been praying for you since Peter

111

wrote to me. "How is Peter?", she enquired. "Would you believe - I haven't laid eyes on him since he left the Seminary and have had only the one letter - but I hope that is the beginning of a renewed friendship. To answer your question - he seems fine...he is settled in to a good job involving horses at a famous Stud Farm in Wexford." "Has he a girlfriend?" she then enquired of Paddy. Paddy suddenly remembered the contents of the letter he had received from Peter and the married women he had had affairs with. "Oh - I suppose several - safety in numbers, they say, is the best motto for a young man." They both laughed as he poured out the tea and offered her the plate of sandwiches. "His mother, Nora, is getting married again soon - I'm delighted for her - she's still a young woman." He then informed her that Peter had been to Killavone recently to see the family. "I have applied to get my job back in the Civil Service, but I don't know yet what their decision will be," she told him. Paddy then asked her if she would be seeing the boyfriend, James, again. "Definitely not," she told him. "Don't call that evil so and so a boyfriend of mine - the way he treated me. He used me, Paddy, and I fell for his charms - but I have no feelings whatsoever for him now - I hope that I never lay eyes on him again," she said with emotion. "I can understand how you feel," said Paddy. "You can now get on with your life and please always remember that you have me as a friend." She interrupted him by saying "Thank you - why do nice fellows like you have to become priests?" Paddy laughed, and said, "I'm not one yet - I'm ninety per cent one if you like - and this is my opportunity to invite you to my ordination ceremony. "I'll be delighted and privileged to be there," she said, as he got up to leave. He asked her to pray for him in this his final furlong to ordination. "I will pray for you every day, Rosa-

112

leen," he told her. "I have your picture to remind me every time I open my breviary," he said, as he held it out to her. "I'd better be off - I have a train to catch or I might be locked out," he laughed. "I have to obey the rules, you know." She seemed very happy as she walked to the Convent door with him. "Keep in touch," he told her. "You know where I am - remember you are the sister I never had," he repeated. When he had left, she rushed down the corridor to Sr. Bridget, Matt Riordan's sister, and told her of his visit and the hope and confidence he had given her. "He'll make a great young priest," the Sister said.

# Chapter 25

The Stage Musical 'Oklahoma' was the show chosen by the Orpheus Musical Society for the new season and Catherine was excited that Peter had agreed to be cast in the lead part of CURLEY, a happy-go-lucky cowboy, opposite herself as LAUREY who, according to the story line is in love with him. Her work in the show was cut out for her, having been cast in a leading part while doubling as the musical's producer. 'Oklahoma' in some strange way had a fascination for her now that she was in love with Peter, her leading man in the show. She wondered should she do in real life with him what the story in the show demanded? Should she find a 'Jud Fry' to take her out and thus make him realise that she musn't be taken for granted? She pondered the wisdom of playing with his emotions and decided against it. She had put all that behind her, now that she was truly in love for the very first time in her life.

During the first night's rehearsals, Peter cut a great dash with the rest of the cast, his beautiful voice adding greatly to his performance. His acting ability, too, was superb and Catherine couldn't believe her luck at such a 'find' for the show. As she put the cast through their paces, she wondered how many in the company knew of her real life love affair with her leading man. She was very much in love with him; of that she had no doubt and she also felt reassured of Peter's devotion were she to judge by the number of times he brought her flowers and told her how much he needed her. The show provided the ideal opportunity for both of them to be together more often and they took full advantage of it. Catherine, who in previous shows, acted as the rehearsal pianist, found it difficult to find a replacement, now that she was taking the part of Laurey. On discussing her problem with Peter, she was reminded that his friend in the Seminary, Paddy Morrissey, was an accomplished musician although, they both felt, in his final months before ordination, getting involved in a show of this nature would be far from his mind. They were to be proved wrong, however, when they telephoned him at "Broadlands" to discuss it with him. He was honoured to be asked, he told them, and even though he couldn't attend rehearsals regularly, he would be happy for Catherine to let him have the musical score and he would attend rehearsals when circumstances permitted. She was pleased with this arrangement and vowed that this particular production of 'Oklahoma' would win as many accolades as possible. She was no stranger to musical awards, for her performances as well as productions; only two years previously, she had won the Association's best Female Singer Award. She felt, this year, the more she watched Peter perform, that he stood a great chance of scooping an accolade, even on his very first outing. No, she wasn't biased, she reminded herself. Peter was a fine performer and was a great asset to the show. He introduced many of his friends to the Society, some of whom were made very welcome members of the gentlemen's chorus, others as back-stage hands. Matt Riordan was delighted to be offered the job in charge of props and his wife Mai busied herself in the administration section, preferring to keep away from the footlights.

Catherine was sad that Jerome, an old stalwart of the Society for the past two productions, would not be performing on this occasion; he had far more serious matters to contend with.

# Chapter 26

When the case against Jerome came up for hearing at the Assizes, it was argued by the State Prosecutors that under the Companies Fraudulent Trading Act, the partners in Dunley Financial Services would be held personally responsible for debts in excess of £100,000, the main creditors being the Irish State, for unpaid Taxes. The company's directors names were read out in court as "Jerome Dunley, at present serving a prison sentence in another jurisdiction for serious offences, Monique de Rocquefort (or Dunley), the common law wife of Jerome Dunley and Clark Beswell, a substantial business man of Co. Wexford." Peter and Catherine were in court to hear the judge announce that "sentencing will be deferred in lieu of a financial settlement which would be made effective by the sale of Dunley Financial Services, a company with assets exceeding the debt." Peter turned to Catherine, and whispering into her ear said, "In layman's language does this mean that Monique or Clark will not be going to jail?" She nodded to him that that was so. Jerome's situation, however, was quite different. He had been sentenced to three years for his part in a money laundering operation as a partner in the Singland Trust, a company that had illegal dealings with a drug smuggling cartel from South East Asia. In pleading guilty to his part in the shady dealings, the judge told him that he was imposing, the minimum sentence and it was to his credit that he had exposed this unscrupulous gang of villains.

Peter was surprised to learn in court, that Jerome and Monique were not lawfully married and couldn't understand why Monique would not have mentioned this to him. He wanted to clear up the matter in his own mind by asking Catherine what the judge meant by 'common law wife'. "It merely means," she told him with a certain satisfaction in her voice, "that they were just living together as man and wife - didn't you ever wonder how Jerome came by his wealth?" "How?" demanded Peter. "I'll tell you how - Monique is still lawfully married to a French Count named Comte de Rocquefort, an ageing gentleman who lives in Normandy. He would never agree to a divorce but gave her a very large amount of money with which she and Jerome set up their Dunley Enterprises." "Thank you for clearing this up - I must say that I wondered for some time which bank Jerome had robbed to be as wealthy as he is," laughed Peter in reply.

Catherine told Monique and Peter that Clark would be arriving from the Middle East shortly and would be examining the implications of the court case. He had been very badly stung by his venture with Jerome and Dunley Finance and would be endeavouring to visit H.M. Wormwood Scrubs Prison in West London before his return to Ireland.

In view of the situation, Monique asked Peter if he would sever his ties with the Beswells in favour of managing Dunley Enterprises, a company not affected by the case. She invited him to come and visit her to discuss it. When he called at her house, he thought she looked absolutely radiant in her blue silk dress, even though it was now quite noticeable that she was heavily pregnant with their child. "Lovely to see you," she told him as she embraced him on his arrival. "Are you proud of the fact that you are going to be a Daddy?" She moved close to him and said "Just imagine, our child will be over two years old when Jerome is released from prison." Peter shuddered at the thought, but did not reveal his feelings. He felt frightened at the implications of what she had just said. He felt that the onus was on him to lend a helping hand while Jerome was out of circulation. "I am asking you, Peter, to manage the company for me - the salary will be substantial and you can live here with me - where you should be - while we await our child." He didn't know how to answer her but finally said "I feel it my duty to help in any way I can, but what would Jerome think if he knew that I was living here with you?" "I'm sure that he would be pleased that his cousin would be looking after his interests," she replied, and then said "Honestly, Peter, I fear for his safety while he is in prison - the unsavoury characters that he became involved with were his undoing. He spilled the beans on them and he will pay for it, I fear. I even worry about my own safety here now." "For God's sake, don't be silly," Peter reassured her. "That's all very well," she said. "I know that they're not all behind bars." Peter then assured her that he would see to it that everything would be done to help but he couldn't give up his job with the Beswells - it was the job he loved and Clark had hinted that he would be promoted shortly. She told him that Jerome was very hurt when he knew that Peter was having an affair with Catherine. "I couldn't care less what he thinks. Catherine and I..." he broke off..."Go on, say it...are in love...Is that it? Go on say it." "Yes, Monique, I'm saying it...Catherine and I are very much in love." "Good God," she cried "have you gone crazy? She is as old as your mother." "I don't care - age doesn't come into it." She couldn't contain her fury any longer. "You told me that you loved me and that's why I'm expecting your baby...do you even appreciate that?" "Monique, if it's possible to love two women - then I love both of you." "Get out of here - and don't ever darken this door again," she screamed at him while he tried to reason with her that he would do everything in his

119

power to help her but that he would keep his job at Kerrigart Stud.

After he left Monique's house he went directly to Catherine's and told her what had transpired. "We will all help her, Peter," she said. "She is under severe strain at present, what with the expected baby and Jerome's problems..." He stopped her by telling her that he was the father of the child... "I knew that darling," she told him. "Nobody told me - I just knew it - call it a woman's intuition...call it what you like...but I knew." "Are you ready for bed?", he asked her, as he took her in his arms and led her upstairs. They undressed each other. "I'm leaving these on..." she teased, pointing to her underwear..."for you to take off me." He lay down beside her and vowed that he would love her forever and ever. She pressed herself close to him and kissed him... "Make it last forever tonight, darling," she pleaded with him.

# Chapter 27

Clark Beswell was kept waiting at least an hour at the prison before he was allowed to see Jerome. A warder had ushered him into a grubby room they called the reception area, where he waited until a woman in a black uniform called him over to the desk by the staircase. "What's your business?", she enquired brusquely. "I have come to see Mr. Dunley," said Clark warily. "We have no Misters here except the Governor - have you his number?" "I'm afraid I don't understand - how do you mean?" She ran her thumb down a list on the desk before asking him if Dunley was a recent arrival. "Ah, yes - Dunley J. Write this down, would you, for future reference. No. 487569." Clark pulled out his pocket diary and entered the number just as a prison warder appeared and walked over to the desk. "The prisoner you have come to see is in the exercise yard - when the bell rings," he said, "they will be returning to their cells." He asked Clark to accompany him up a flight of stairs, down a long corridor, across a landing where they were looking down on a courtyard. A large group of men were lining up in formation to march back to their cells. Clark thought he could see Jerome at the back of the line. "Wait here," the warder said, "a guard will take you down to the visiting area." Suddenly, he heard the sound of metal as a burly, young-looking uniformed guard arrived, with a bunch of giant keys hanging from his right arm. They walked down another flight of stairs and met Jerome coming towards them, flanked by a warder. He looked a pitiful sight in his prison grey overalls and shaven head. He had always taken such a pride in his plentiful, curly black hair and must have been humiliated to have been shorn in this fashion. "You have just seven minutes,'' shouted the warder, ''- make the most of it, Paddy.'' Jerome stared at the warder indignantly and turned to Clark seated opposite him with a mesh grille separating them. ''I am incensed to have taken this kind of a rap - I have been set up by those Mafia bastards - I named the one's in court who should be in here instead of me - someone shouted from the gallery that they'd get me - I don't care anymore,'' he roared.

Clark broke into his harangue ''You got the very minimum sentence for coming clean on the whole thing - and pleading guilty.'' Clark had hardly finished when Jerome blurted out ''For Christ's sake, man - three bloody years - that's what I got, three bloody years.'' ''That means two years with good behaviour,'' volunteered Clark weakly. ''We waited ten years for a baby and now look where I am - the kid will be a couple of years old by the time I get out of this fucking place.'' Clark tried to console him by saying that Monique would be well looked after in the meantime. ''What bloody good is that to me, rotting in here?'' The prison warder broke up the conversation by saying ''O.K. Paddy, your visit's over - time up, let's go.'' Jerome jumped to his feet, turned his back on Clark, walked swiftly through the double doors in front of him and disappeared down a corridor. Clark, meanwhile, tried to compose himself and walked up the staircase and across the corridor and down the other stairs towards the main door where his taxi was waiting. He was relieved to be breathing fresh air again and as he got into the back seat of the cab, said to the driver - ''Ever been in there?'' ''No, Guv - nor do I want to - they say the food isn't great either,'' he joked as he started up the engine. ''Take me to Heathrow Airport - I have to catch a flight to Ireland.'' He settled into the back seat and pondered the fate of the hapless Jerome, and compared it with his own good fortune. Within a matter of hours, he would be meeting members of the Irish Government who would be preparing press releases for the media on his breakthrough in the Middle Eastern and French markets for the Irish Bloodstock Agency. It was a huge stroke of good fortune for him and for Irish exports to those regions. Here he was, on the threshold of a major international breakthrough for Irish Bloodstock, while his partner in another venture would languish in jail for the next three years. He felt lucky that he had not met Jerome three years earlier when he might have been tempted to have become involved with the Singland Trust, the British company which had brought disaster and ruin to his friend. He would, no doubt, pay dearly in monetary terms as a result of the court case in Ireland, but anything was preferable to what he had witnessed during his prison visit.

# Chapter 28

The notices had been erected all over the South East - "The Orpheus Musical Society presents for their 4th Production, 'OKLAHOMA', a Musical Comedy by Richard Rodgers and Oscar Hammerstein, produced and choreographed by CATHERINE BESWELL". Peter was ecstatic to see his name and that of Catherine on every hoarding in the County; "The Part of CURLEY to be played by newcomer, Peter Dunley opposite Catherine Beswell as LAUREY". He thought it so coincidental that the characters in the show played by both of them, are in love with each other and he also wondered if there were many productions staged where the leading parts were played by real life lovers; he had read of cases in the cinema where the participants fell in love. His situation, however, was unique, to be playing in the show with the woman he loved and marrying her before the final curtain, and it excited them both greatly.

It was fever pitch as Sunday night's opening approached. There was the matinee in the afternoon which would iron out any hitches and he was delighted that Paddy had come for the week of rehearsals, augmented by the arrival of Rosaleen. There was euphoria when Peter heard the good news. This was the very first time he had laid eyes on her since her visit to the Seminary and her subsequent miscarriage. Paddy and herself were invited to stay at Beswells but Peter arranged that Paddy would stay with Monique at a time when she most needed moral support. She was now seven months pregnant with Peter's baby, a fact not known to either Paddy or Rosaleen and that's the way he wanted it. He hoped that he wouldn't be overcome with nerves for his first night's performance now that his close friends would also be in the audience. This year, Catherine told him, she was departing from the usual format of previous shows by having him come out before curtain-up and introduce the show to the audience. He would, of course, have to wear a dress suit for this special duty, an item that he did not possess, he informed her. "I have seen just the suit for you, darling," she assured him, "at Richie's Department Store - we'll go there tomorrow and on this occasion we should find the time to increase this famous wardrobe of yours." Peter remembered that the last time they went to town to do just this, they had to return almost immediately when they learned from the morning papers that Jerome had been arrested.

The final dress rehearsal performed before an invited audience went very well but according to Catherine, wasn't vibrant enough. She didn't want any second-rate performances from any of her players - she wanted their best shots every night until the final curtain. She also advised the cast of the likelihood of adjudicators assessing the individual performances of the players as the week went by. She had set her mind on an award for the production this season as well as the possibility that Peter might win the best newcomer trophy. She was convinced that, with the appropriate tuition, he could turn professional.

Peter hardly slept a wink on Saturday night with the thought of the matinee at 3 pm on Sunday. When he arrived, the hall was filling up rapidly with noisy youngsters, many of them accompanied by their parents. He stood backstage and observed, through a crack in the side curtain, the people taking their seats and he felt the adrenalin surge through his body. He decided to keep his introduction, as arranged by Catherine, until the main performance, when Clark, Monique, Rosaleen would be occupying the front seats and Paddy Morrissey would be down in the pit with the orchestra 'performing his magic' as Catherine described it. She was enchanted with the rehearsals and felt that if Paddy led them in this fashion throughout the week, then she would have no problems in that department.

It was rapidly approaching 3 pm. The hall was full to capacity; there was an air of excitement and expectancy about the building and backstage was electric. Suddenly, Catherine beckoned to Peter to get out there and introduce the show. According to the female members of the show, he looked immaculate in his fabulous new dress suit, with blue bow tie and matching handkerchief and Catherine was obviously delighted. Before he ventured out, he had one final squint through a crack in the curtain, composed himself, lifted the corner of the main curtain and appeared in front of the packed house. He walked right up to the footlights. "My Lord Bishop, Reverend Fathers," he began, having spotted members of the clergy being escorted to their front seats. "Ladies and Gentlemen, tonight the Orpheus Musical Society, composed of the talent of this region, presents for your pleasure and your critical acclaim, a Musical Comedy set in American Indian Territory at the turn of the Century." He paused and glanced at the programme that he held tightly rolled in his hands. He knew that everything he wanted to say by way of introduction was there but Catherine had warned him not to read from it. He recovered quickly and in a slightly faltering voice continued "The story goes something like this - Laurey, played by the lovely Catherine Beswell, our Producer, is in love with Curley, played by myself; She decides to make him jealous by accepting an invitation from Jud Fry to go to a show. Her action causes bitterness between Jud and myself but in the end everything turns out alright and I marry her." There was thunderous applause as he searched for something to say, when he heard Catherine behind the curtain whispering to him "That's enough - that's enough, - take a bow and come in." He told the audience that the rest of the story they would have to work out for themselves. He rushed backstage as the orchestra struck up the opening numbers from the show, and quickly prepared for his own part in the production.

They played to packed houses all week with powerful performances that improved nightly much to Catherine's satisfaction. When the show completed its successful run in the South East, Peter was absolutely delighted to learn that the Committee had decided to bring it to the other Provinces and they would be playing shortly in Peter's own village at the Church Hall at Killavone. He had been on the stage there in his youth during Christmas concerts but now he would be playing with a well-known Musical Society in front of his own people. He was thrilled at the prospect.

# Chapter 29

The month of May was a particularly busy one for the Dunleys; there was Paddy's ordination to the priesthood at "Broadlands" Seminary, an immensely important occasion to which they were privileged to have been invited. Nora had postponed her 'big day' so as to have their newly ordained friend officiate at her wedding to Bert Flanagan. Killavone Parish Church of Saint Bridget was chosen for the wedding, as it had been nearly thirty years previously when Nora walked down the aisle with Peter's late father, John Dunley, when she was barely twenty years old.

The Church was packed to capacity for the ceremony, not all of them invited guests, but parishioners eager to get a glimpse of the bride taking marriage vows for the second time. There was a hush in the congregation as Canon Jim turned to Nora and asked her if she would take Albert Flanagan as her lawful wedded husband. Many of them in the church were present on that Sunday morning when, after the Canon had read out the banns, a lady at the back shouted that Bertie was her husband. The priest was badly shaken by the experience and had taken extra precautions to examine church records subsequently, so that there would not be a repetition of that most unpleasant incident. During the ceremony Peter thought to himself that if he had remained in the Seminary until ordination, he would more than likely be standing there in Father Paddy's place marrying his own mother!

Monique was restless throughout the ceremony and complained quietly to Peter beside her, that she was in some discomfort. Her doctor had advised against the long journey in view of her baby's imminent arrival. She had braved the journey, nevertheless, to be present at his mother's wedding. When the priests observed her distress, they halted the service to ask if the local Doctor was in the church. No sooner was the announcement made than the local nurse was on hand to direct operations and Monique was ushered out and quickly taken to the Priest's house next door, and an ambulance summoned from nearby Kilmaine district hospital.

The wedding guests, meanwhile, were making their way to the Provincial Hotel in Kilmaine where the wedding breakfast was booked. Before the ambulance arrived, Monique, assisted by the nurse had given birth to 'a bouncing baby boy' as they described him afterwards to the guests. She was soon on her way to the hospital's maternity ward accompanied by Father Paddy and Peter, both of whom were still in a state of shock having been present during the birth of the baby. Neither of them had ever experienced a situation like this before, and when they arrived at the hospital, the nurse called them aside and in mock admonishment said "You both look as if you yourselves had had the baby and not the wee girl in the ward. If the men witnessed more of these situations, they might be a bit more understanding of the women." Peter interrupted to remind her that she had never had a baby herself. "True for you young man," she answered, "I'm an old hand at this job though - for nearly forty years I have been bringing children into the world including yourself," she said, pointing to him. Nurse Madden had never married but had the proud distinction of having delivered three generations of babies' into one particular family in the parish of Killavone. "I can't understand it," she went on, "look at the two of you, in a total state of shock for having witnessed the most natural thing in the world - the birth of a baby. Go on now, boys, and enjoy yourselves at the wedding -

as for me, I have more work to do.'' Before they left the hospital, Peter turned to Father Paddy and with tears of joy streaming down his face, told him that he was the father of the baby they had just seen born into the world. Father Paddy put a hand on his shoulder and said to him just three words "I partly guessed." They walked briskly across town to the Provincial Hotel where they called for two double whiskies in the front bar before entering the function room where the invited guests were being seated for the meal. They took their places at the top table as the Canon asked them to stand for 'Grace before meals'. When everyone was re-seated, he leant across the table to Peter and asked him what the news was from the hospital. "Is it a boy or a girl?", he enquired of Peter quietly, as he tucked his serviette under his ample collar in preparation for the enormous meal.

# Chapter 30

No sooner had the toast been proposed to the future happiness of Nora and Bertie, than the Canon was on his feet again to say the 'Grace after meals' and to make two important announcements. "Before the customary speeches that accompany a wedding, I have two very important announcements to make," he began. "It is always a joyous occasion to officiate at the wedding of a parishioner and good friend, but today the joy is twofold in announcing that Mrs. Jerome Dunley has given birth to a bouncing baby boy and all within minutes of Nora's wedding to Bertie." Amidst the thunderous applause of the hundred or so guests he went on "There is sadness, too, that her husband Jerome cannot be here but I ask all of you to pray for his happiness and that he will be home soon again and re-united with his family." Peter had a shattering thought while the priest was on his feet. What would the priest say, he wondered, if he knew that Jerome and Monique were not married in the eyes of the Catholic Church and how would he react if he knew who the real father of Monique's child was? What would have transpired, if the true facts were known by Canon Jim Mulraney, didn't even bear thinking about!

After Peter had congratulated his mother and Bertie, his thoughts turned to his new born son across the town in the district hospital and he wanted to be there as soon as possible. Meanwhile, the festivities had to be enjoyed and he was well aware that he would soon be asked to perform some of the songs he was well known for as a young lad in the Christmas concerts at Killavone. Canon Jim was now on stage making what he called his second announcement. "Ladies and Gentlemen," he commenced,

"I hope you can all hear me." He tugged at the microphone lead and brushed it behind his feet before continuing. "We are indeed privileged to have The Orpheus Musical Society - all the way from the other end of the country in their final performance of this year, coming to this very parish of Killavone - to our Church Hall to be exact, to present their show 'Oklahoma'. It is, indeed, a great occasion for the parish," he went on, "to be considered for a show of this magnitude and our grateful thanks must go to the young man here beside me," - he beckoned to Peter to come on stage - "Peter Dunley, who is, I understand, starring in the show." To rapturous applause Peter acknowledged the guests by bowing graciously. "And the proceeds of these shows," Canon Jim said, when the applause had died down, "are being kindly donated to the Parish Hall Fund. Our Hall has yet to be paid for," he reminded them, "so I don't want an empty seat at the matinee or the night's main performance." He was a priest well known for his fund-raising and would milk this opportunity for all that it was worth at every mass prior to the event. "In conclusion, can I ask Nora and Bertie to lead the dancers on the floor while Peter sings us a couple of waltz medleys." Finally he replaced the microphone on its stand and left the stage before Peter obliged with a couple of old favourites that had the assembled guests bewitched.

# Chapter 31

Rosaleen returned to Wexford with Peter and Father Paddy after the wedding festivities were complete, while Monique remained at Kilmaine Hospital to recuperate. Rosaleen was thrilled to be taking up her new position as secretary to the Beswells, an important post that Peter had secured for her. Her arrival there coincided with the communique from the Government that her new boss, Clark Beswell, was invited to oversee the formation of the country's National Bloodstock Council. "Ireland would be forever indebted to him," the Government Press Release stated, "for his generosity, knowledge and expertise in the equestrian world and for having created such potential opportunities for bloodstock exports."

Before he left home to join the team of civil servants that were accompanying him on their overseas export mission, he summoned Peter to his office, to brief him on various business details of Kerrigart and to familiarise him with business negotiations that would soon be taking place at home. "Some time ago," he began, "I mentioned to you that big things were in the offing for our business." Peter listened to him intently, wondering what was coming next. He noticed, too, that Rosaleen in her office in an annexe to Clark's was within earshot of their conversation and it made him feel good. Clark reached behind him to the drinks cabinet, poured a whiskey for both of them and continued, "I have followed your progress with considerable interest and have every confidence that you can fill my shoes so to speak, while I'm overseas on this important mission." "Thank you, Clark. I will endeavour to see that everything runs smoothly while you are away and may I too wish you every success."

Clark looked pleased and continued "It is an exciting venture...after France we go to Egypt where we will be guests of the Cairo Government. Keep the press cuttings for me," he joked. "By the way," Clark said, as he walked across to Rosaleen's desk "this young lady has the makings of a good secretary - is she your girlfriend?" "She was," said Peter, as Rosaleen tossed back her beautiful blonde locks and looked at both of them shyly. "Look after Catherine too while I am out of the country - she thinks a lot of you; I'm sure you know that yourself." Peter felt uneasy at this last remark about Catherine; it was the way he looked at him while saying it. Perhaps it was Peter's guilt complex; or maybe Clark really did know about their relationship and was merely turning a blind eye to the whole business. Whatever he thought, Catherine certainly did not now seem to care that more and more people, especially employees, knew that they were seeing quite a lot of each other. He felt that he should tell Rosaleen, now that she was ensconced as his secretary in Clark's absence. It was all so unreal, he felt, to be suddenly acting Managing Director in this large organisation with Rosaleen by his side.

Catherine had been invited to accompany her husband with the Government delegation but had turned down the invitation in the company's business interests. She drove Clark to Dublin before returning home next evening. During the drive back to Wexford, she was fully aware of the importance of Clark's export mission and the lucrative possibilities that it would ultimately open up for their own company. She decided that the time was right to reward Peter financially for his loyalty and dedication, and what an appropriate time she felt, on the eve of his birthday to be rewarding him with a considerable hike in his salary. He would be twenty-five years of age by the time she saw him again. They had arranged to go out to dinner on her return, to celebrate his birthday in style and she worked out as she drove leisurely through the countryside the outfit she would wear that he would like for their dinner appointment.

Peter was waiting anxiously when she drove directly to his apartment to collect him. He was wearing his new, dark blue double-breasted suit with brilliant white shirt and matching tie when he opened the hall door of the flat to greet her. He thought she looked fabulous and told her so. "I haven't even changed yet," she laughed. "Spare the compliments until you see me in my new dress." They drove to her home where she dressed for this special occasion.

They detoured to their local pub before continuing on to town where they had booked a table for two in the quietest corner of their favourite restaurant in the Tropicana Hotel, a recently built luxury hotel on the outskirts of the town. Later that night, Catherine drove them back to her home where they spent the night together. "You are twenty-five darling," she said to him as she undressed for bed. "Are you wondering what I bought you?" She watched him in the dressing table mirror as he stepped out of his trousers. He pulled her close to him and undid her bra to reveal her beautiful breasts. He kissed them gently at first and then sank to his knees to kiss her lovely body. After laying her down on the giant four-poster bed he continued to undress her. As he revealed himself to her she said to him "Is all this mine?" She murmured how much she wanted him as she helped slip his underpants down his manly thighs. Lying down beside her, she in turn kissed him all over and drew him on top of her as she opened her luscious thighs to him. "It is your turn, sweetheart," she whispered in his ear, "kiss me the way I love being kissed." He drove her wild with desire before laying his body on hers and thrusting himself into her. He loved her passionately, telling her how beautiful she looked tonight and how much he would always love and cherish her. After she had trembled in a powerful climax, he lay beside her, revelling in her beauty and could not believe that she was nearly twenty years his senior - almost as old as his own mother, as Monique had reminded him angrily when she first suspected them of being lovers.

# Chapter 32

The National newspapers were reporting that these were exciting days for Clark Beswell, heading up the Irish Export Trade Mission to France, and the Government Press Secretary, in a briefing to senior journalists at the Irish Embassy in Paris hailed it as a huge success. The Trade Minister had joined them for a photo-call opportunity before their onward leg of a journey that would take them to Cairo in Egypt and, hopefully, to other nations in the Arab League which had been formed at the end of World War 2. Beswell was well aware that, if they could clench the Egyptian deal it could be the first of many with the six other Arab States in the League. He had enormous empathy with all the Arabs with whom he had talks and had found the Egyptians, in particular, to be great judges of the equine species; indeed, he had often remarked that the well-bred Arab stallion and the Irish thoroughbred mare were the perfect mating combination for quality racehorses. The Irish Delegation were duly wished a ''Bon Voyage'' by their French hosts and their Super Constellation aircraft took off at 1700 hours, en route to Cairo via Marseilles, in what seemed to be ideal weather conditions.

Approximately ninety minutes into the flight an aircraft controller from a French Air Base at St Etienne in the Massif Central reported that he had picked up a distress signal from what was later confirmed as having come from the Irish pilot of the stricken aircraft who radioed that he was attempting to climb out of extreme turbulence by a violent thunderstorm. That was the only message received from the ill-fated airliner since they had become airborne. Marseilles Airport control reported the aircraft missing from their radar screens and all aircraft were alerted to look out for it.

Several days later, a French light aircraft reported the sighting of wreckage strewn over the side of a mountain peak of the Jura range, inside the Swiss border, which was later confirmed as the missing airliner carrying Clark Beswell and his export trade mission.

Catherine appeared, devastated, on Peter's arm when the remains of the delegation and crew of the airliner were flown in to Dublin Airport for burial. Huge crowds lined the streets from the airport to the cemetery in a final tearful farewell to "Clark Beswell and the team of Government personnel who had so tragically lost their lives in the air disaster" as the Taoiseach described them in an oration at the communal plot where their remains were finally laid to rest.

Catherine had been advised in advance that formal identification of her husband would have proved impossible, the remains had been so badly charred in the inferno which had claimed their lives. There were certain personal belongings that had to be claimed by the next of kin, however. The only item of Clark's belongings that was identifiable was a gold pocket-watch and chain which Catherine had given her late husband on the anniversary of their first meeting. That poignant memento was later inlaid in a monument erected to the memory of Clark Beswell at the entry to his beloved Kerrigart Stud Farm. The irony of that ill-fated Trade Mission led by Beswell was that, had they arrived in Cairo, they would have been embroiled in the Coup D'Etat that overthrew the Egyptian King during that same week of 1952. The Trade Mission was successfully resumed in 1956, on this occasion led by Peter Dunley, after Gamal Abdel Nasser became President.

# Chapter 33

In the aftermath of the horrific air disaster that claimed her husband's life, Catherine realised how traumatised the employees of the Beswell Group really were, at the sudden demise of their boss, who had been held in such high esteem by every member of the staff. She had convened a meeting of management and workers to explain that business had to carry on as normal "that is the way a professional like Clark" as she described him, "would have wished it, in the interests of the company." She then formally introduced Peter Dunley who would, she explained, be assuming Clark's mantle and was being installed as the Company's Managing Director. "All of you who have had dealings with Peter during my late husband's absence, when business interests took him overseas so often, will know that he is capable of running our business interests now that we have suffered such a tragic loss with the death of my husband and we pray that he will go from strength to strength in capitalising on the many opportunities out there awaiting us if we interpret them correctly for the benefit of all of us in the future." She then invited Peter to speak, who, after first calling for a minute's silence in honour of their late boss, told the gathering that it was Clark Beswell who had given him his first break. "It is hard to come to terms with the fact that a man of his considerable talents and calibre could so suddenly be taken from us in such a horrific fashion - a man larger than life, so to speak, who had so much to give to the country as well as to his business." He delivered these words with considerable conviction and without a hint of emotion apparent in his voice, and was about to continue when Catherine interrupted his train of thought by handing him a letter she had received from the Government Department of Communications and which stated that "the official result of the French Government inquiry into the air disaster would soon be made available but that the preliminary investigations seemed to confirm that the airliner had been struck by lightning and the pilot had veered off course, having lost his instrumentation, before crashing into the Jura Mountains." As he finished reading that sombre letter, he noticed that many employees were quietly sobbing into their handkerchiefs and he knew that he had a hard act to follow in filling Clark's shoes. He couldn't help but notice, in contrast to the obvious distress apparent in many of the employees present, the lack of emotion in Catherine's face as she sat next to him in the boardroom. Before concluding, he looked across at Rosaleen and introduced her to the staff as his new secretary and when he announced that "the tried and trusted Matt Riordan" was to be promoted from Estates to General Manager, there was obvious approval that Matt was being rewarded for his loyal service to Beswell over so many years.

As the staff filed out of the building, a groom was heard to enquire of another how long it would now take before Peter and Catherine 'made it legal' and announced that they would be 'tying the knot'. They were prophetic words indeed - within six months Peter Dunley married Catherine Beswell in a civil ceremony in Northern Ireland, news that was received with incredulity by members of his family and which echoed what Monique had told him once, in a jealous rage, that "Catherine was old enough to be his mother." She, too, was stunned when they both arrived at her home to announce that they were getting married. It was the natural thing to do, Catherine explained, now that Peter held considerable equity in the Company and was effectively in total control of the organisation. Monique, who had been about to ask them to accompany her to London to visit the hapless Jerome, holed up in Wormwood Scrubs, felt now that it would not be advisable, given this latest set of circumstances. She wondered if he knew of the tragic events surrounding Clark given the huge media coverage that the disaster had provoked. He wasn't allowed a radio in his cell but received the occasional newspaper.

# Chapter 34

Monique had only just returned from Normandy where her aged husband Comte De Rocquefort had been laid to rest in the family crypt below the high altar of the town's cathedral where the remains of his ancestors lay in their caskets of lead. She had been left comfortably off, with the residue of his Estate after the considerable death duties had been paid. This was extremely good news for her as Dunley Enterprises had continued to falter since the incarceration of Jerome with whom she had had an unhappy relationship, particularly in recent years. She was disillusioned at the manner in which he had squandered most of her original fortune in his sometimes bizarre business ventures, culminating now in its near bankruptcy. She, naturally, felt sorry for him but had now reached a time in her life when she was at her happiest, now that she had a beautiful young son to provide for and a nice windfall of cash and property bequeathed to her, with which to do so. She dreaded the visit to Jerome in prison and having to lie to him about the true identity of her son but her fear was short-lived when, on the very eve of her proposed departure, she received a telegram from H.M. Prison Authorities "regretting that prisoner No. 487569 has been found unconscious in his cell sometime after his return there, having had a visit from a male purporting to be a relative of his. The prisoner is currently in the intensive care unit in the medical wing of the prison and no further visits can be allowed until further advised." Scarcely twenty four hours after that solemn announcement, Monique received the sad news that Jerome had passed away and that an enquiry would be held as to the circumstances of his death.

Peter was shattered to learn that Jerome was dead, only a few short months after Clark, both of them having suffered such tragic ends within such a short space of time. It was eerie, he thought. Jerome must have been got at by his enemies, he pondered, as there was no way that he would have died by his own hand. He and Monique would be travelling to the Prison to claim the body for burial when they hoped to learn further details of his tragic end. Monique, having recovered from the dreadful initial shock of having received the terrible news, was now, in a way quite relieved. This was the end of Dunley Enterprises and all that was left was for the mechanism of Receivership to be put in motion.

Her public persona, when she first contacted Peter with the sad news, was somewhat different, however. "This is the end of Jerome and his crumbled empire," she told him tearfully, and when she regained her composure she reminded him that they both shared guilt in the deception they had engaged in when he was alive. "But good has come out of it all, Peter," she argued, "we have a lovely son from our relationship which would not have happened but for Jerome - you know what I mean, Peter - he is your son too - please come and see him soon - I really would relish that - he will have to get to know his daddy, won't he?" Peter did not reply; he was too preoccupied by the responsibilities suddenly thrust upon him of acting for the Dunley family and to make sure that Jerome had a decent burial.

# Chapter 35

On the Sunday afternoon, there was quite a crowd of locals, consisting mainly of women with their children, outside the church of St. Bonaventure, eager to catch a glimpse of Monique and her baby as they arrived for the baptismal service. It was no ordinary arrival either; Peter had ensured that by arranging that Matt Riordan, dressed as a liveryman, would tackle up the two white Irish Draught horses to the landau carriage from the Estate courtyard and carry them in style to the church door. The late Clark Beswell had acquired a collection of vintage coaches and carriages, many of them priceless specimens, with which he had intended opening a museum to the public on the estate if God had spared him a while longer.

Peter and Rosaleen were nominated as godparents to the newborn and chosen as sponsors at the baptism, Peter's role in the ceremony being unique in the Catholic church, given that he was also the child's father! Rosaleen accompanied Monique in the horse drawn carriage to the church, both of them looking radiant as they alighted from the vehicle to the envious gaze of the local onlookers.

The Dunley family and some close relatives had made the long journey to Wexford for the happy event which was followed by a social function for the guests that went on into the early hours of Monday morning. Father Paddy Morrissey was invited to perform the baptismal service, his first as an ordained priest. After the service, the family and guests lined up for the photographer, Peter and Monique standing proudly in front with their newly baptised secret love child accompanied by Rosaleen and Father Morrissey, his arm resting gently around her shoulders. As the guests entered the hotel lobby, many of them noticed with disapproval that the cleric held hands with the lovely Rosaleen as they strode in together seemingly oblivious of everyone. "It was just not right," an elderly Aunt of Peter's recalled later, "that a handsome young priest, barely out of the Seminary would be paying such attention to such an attractive young lady." Later that night as the festivities were well underway, if she had the misfortune to have remained at the party, she would have observed that the young priest and his lovely companion danced all the slow dances cheek-to-cheek fashion and were inseparable as the night wore on. "I never thought I would live to see goings on like it," another guest was heard to remark as he left the function room with his wife. "What is the world coming to? And this is holy Catholic Ireland," the wife added, as they made their exit to the carpark of the hotel. "A Protestant Minister wouldn't do the likes of what we have just witnessed and they are allowed to get married," the husband roared, as they got in the hackney cab that was waiting for them outside!

Peter's new wife, Catherine, had not attended the baptismal ceremony or the festivities afterwards due to illness but was known to be angry when the photographic album of the event was presented to her some days later. She felt very strongly, she told Peter, that the pictures suggested that he and Monique were man and wife judging from the way he had posed with her and the baby. "I am incensed and humiliated by you," she screamed at him. "Have you no sensitivity towards me - your wife, to have posed for those photographs with her, in the manner you did?" She raced upstairs clutching the album and when he followed to reason with her he watched in horror as she ripped it in pieces in an act of total defiance and then defaced the offending pictures. He stood there silently, in a state of total shock and appalled by the tantrum she had thrown. He was beginning to feel that she may soon need medical attention for the obsessive bouts of rage and jealousy, to which she was increasingly prone. He discussed her condition with the priest who rationalised that Catherine was now a victim of circumstances, having, on the one hand, married a man twenty years her junior, and now she was feeling the ignominy of her young husband being the father of her friend's child. She was, he said, also painfully aware that she herself would never be able to bear him a child. "It is a lot for her to take all at once," Father Paddy advised him. "Be gentle and understanding with her; you have an unusual, though not unique, marriage with her and you have, by marrying her, inherited her late husband's wealth; she loves you dearly, Peter, as you well know and you must be more understanding of her feelings." Peter was thankful to him for the advice but re-iterated that he also felt duty bound to look after his young son and heir.

Catherine's anger and frustration were soon quelled with the exciting news that the Orpheus Musical Society and her production of 'OKLAHOMA' had earned them no less than three awards from the Association of Musical Societies. Peter, her pride and joy, she boasted, had scooped the Best Irish Voice Award, while she herself won the coveted Best Amateur Producer Trophy. She was also overjoyed to learn that her show had gained the recognition of being the year's most ambitious musical presentation. Now that Peter was at the helm of the Beswell Group, she felt that she could give more of her time and attention to the casting and production of next year's Musical - she had already pencilled in her diary what it was going to be and had no doubt in her mind who would be taking the male lead in 'The Student Prince'.

# Chapter 36

When the body of Jerome Dunley was finally released from H.M. Prison, Peter was in London to claim it for the return to Ireland by Private Air Charter. Many relatives had journeyed to the Airport to meet the remains on the final journey back to Killavone for burial. It was a sombre occasion as the cortege finally entered the village at a snail's pace to the local church where the body lay overnight in its coffin as was the custom. The following morning, after the funeral service, the coffin was carried from the church and transferred to a horse-drawn hearse for the final leg of the journey to the Dunley family burial vault in the graveyard at Kilrane. The weather was extremely inclement with a strong wind blowing from the South West as the pall bearers drew the coffin from the hearse to carry it shoulder high from the road to the graveyard. As they lifted the casket on to their shoulders, a sudden gust of wind in a final macabre dance of death, lifted the coffin lid clean off its base and as it fell down on the roadside, the pall bearers let down the coffin to retrieve it. There, to their horror, the mourners gathered around, caught a glimpse of Jerome's remains and were left in no doubt as to how he had died. It wasn't a pretty sight as the screams of terror of those who witnessed the gruesome corpse testified. There for all to see were the remains of Jerome with his head partially blown off, revealing the truth that he had indeed been shot by someone at close range in prison. There was deep indignation among the mourners when they recovered their composure, with a number of them expressing their feelings that there had been a cover-up by the British prison authorities. These views, however, were subsequently to be proved incorrect when it was reported that a Prison Officer who was a prime suspect in the murder, had disappeared. An anonymous letter received soon afterwards by Monique, confirmed that certain people named by Jerome in court had exacted their revenge on her late husband. After she had furnished the British authorities with this letter, she was informed that "no stone would be left unturned in bringing those responsible to justice." The Prison Officer responsible was later arrested in Holland and brought back to face the courts where he was convicted of murder and sentenced to hang for his crime, in a case that received wide publicity in Great Britain and Ireland. His sentence was later commuted to life imprisonment.

After Jerome's body was finally laid to rest in the family vault beside the coffin of the late John Dunley, Canon Jim Mulraney was invited to join the family for lunch at the Dunley homestead. Jerome's mother, Annie, by now an infirm old lady in the care of the Old People's Hospice, had been brought along in her wheelchair. She didn't appear to grasp the fact that it was the remains of her only son that had been laid to rest and no one enlightened her. Mercifully, she hadn't been aware of her unfortunate son's previous business problems or jail sentence either. The Canon was livid that the funeral had not gone as smoothly as he would have wished. He was convinced that some maladjusted person had tampered with the coffin lid in gruesome curiosity and he wanted to get to the bottom of it. "I am deeply concerned that some evil person tampered with that coffin, possibly in the church, and I apologise to the family for any distress it caused you - I will have more to say on this from the pulpit on Sunday." He pounded the table with his fist as he continued "The curse of God will fall on the villain who could have done this." The family stayed silent about the event until Peter's brother, Joe, volunteered "It could have been an accident...perhaps they didn't screw the lid on properly when they put the body in." The Canon interrupted him "It was no accident, Joe...yes, I have my suspicions but it will be hard to prove anything. Did anybody see Jimmy at the funeral?" he then enquired. He was referring to the workman who had caused such havoc for Nora after he had discovered that she was about to remarry. There was the letting down of her new man's motorcar tyres and then there was the terrible incident during the reading of the wedding banns. Jimmy would never be forgiven by the Canon and he was again his prime suspect. "I want you all to make your enquiries," he went on - "I will not let this rest," he concluded. Nora finally asked all present "to pray for the repose of Jerome's soul and let him rest in peace." They then left the table and went their separate ways.

The Canon certainly didn't let the matter rest. At Sunday's sermon he enlightened the congregation - at least those who needed enlightening, what had transpired during the burial of the late Jerome and he told them he had made significant headway in determining who the culprit was. This was a ghastly deed, he said, and a sacrilege in the house of God. Jimmy, he found out had indeed been around for the funeral and was convinced that it was his 'morbid curiosity' that caused him to have a final look at Jerome's corpse. If it was him, the Canon said, then he needed treatment fast, before he did something even more sinister.

# Chapter 37

Peter was heartened by the enthusiasm of the Board members about his performance as Managing Director of Beswell and it was adopted that the company, under his guidance would seek the expertise of high profile people in the bloodstock and racing circles with a view to further acquisitions for the firm. His aim now was to increase their company shareholdings in various ventures and to purchase suitable land in strategic locations for stud and racing purposes in Ireland and Great Britain. A new company was formed to oversee this, named Dunley Bloodstock Developments, an organisation that mushroomed rapidly to the extent that within five years it had become the leading and most profitable of its type in Britain and the Continent. Peter Dunley was lauded by his peers in the Bloodstock business and was, within a short time to become a legend in racing circles for his knowledge and foresight in his choice of trainers. His horses were soon winning most of the major racing events at home and overseas, a factor that necessitated considerable extra travel. Monique had invested substantially in the new company and was soon sharing the spoils of success with him. They were seen together at many of the social occasions that went with their success, fuelling speculation that his young marriage to Catherine was on the rocks. These stories reached the gossip columns of the National Newspapers, causing Catherine considerable anguish. When the rumours persisted in the high circulation and sleazy Sunday Echo, she decided to sue. At the same time, unknown to Peter and Monique, she had a private detective agency investigate their movements when Monique accompanied him on a business trip to the North of England. The information that was fed back left her in no doubt but that Peter's affair had been rekindled. She was devastated, naturally, but was advised by the Private Eye to hold her fire until incontrovertible evidence could be provided in Ireland. That evidence soon surfaced in the form of a front page sensational story in the Sunday Empire with a banner headline which read 'Racing Magnate's Loving Partnership'. The scurrilous article went so far as to claim that Monique was pregnant with Peter's second child and that Catherine and himself were living apart. The latter part of the story was untrue; in fact it was in their marriage bed that she confronted him on Sunday morning after she had had her regular morning stroll through the local village where she accidentally picked up a copy of the tabloid newspaper that carried the offending story. She could take no more as she rushed upstairs into the master bedroom where Peter was having his Sunday morning lie in. The row that ensued left the bedroom of their stately home in ruins. She smashed mirrors, attacked his wardrobe and destroyed his shirts, suits and coats; she tore up their wedding album and then lunged at him with a pair of scissors she had grabbed from the dressing table. She narrowly missed as he jumped out of bed and tried vainly to reason with her. She confronted him with her own evidence compiled by the Private eye after he tried to tell her that it was all a newspaper fabrication. She lunged at him again with the scissors screaming obscenities as she careered madly about the bedroom. "Bastard," she screamed, "you dirty, rotten, lousy bastard. You've been cheating on me despite your promises that you would never see her." She continued to scream hysterically as she tried to injure him by throwing two priceless Ming vases in his direction, smashing them in fragments. "I will disfigure you for life, you lousy cheat. I have given you everything," she screamed again and again, finally breaking down in tears as she raced from the bedroom, down the staircase and through the hall into the garden. Peter rushed after her but was not able to stop her as she sped off in her car down the driveway towards the main road. He raced back into the house and telephoned Monique to warn her in case she was on her way there to do her an injury. Monique did not answer the telephone. He hoped that she and the child had gone out in case Catherine in her present state might try to harm either of them. The telephone rang sometime later as he was dressing; it was Monique in a hysterical state..."Catherine has gone off her head," she screamed down the telephone, "...she came here and grabbed little Peter and drove off with him." "Stay where you are," he told her calmly. "I am coming right over." He telephoned the Gardai and told them what had transpired before heading down to Monique's home where she was in an overwrought state. Some time later the police informed them that they had intercepted her car at Sailor's Point, a picturesque spot near the cliffs. They had rescued the child but Catherine had broken away and had fallen into the sea from a height of more than three hundred feet. Despite frantic searches throughout the day by the local lifeboat team, there was no sign of her. The sea was very choppy and had carried her swiftly away. "Please God, Oh please God bring her safely back," shouted Peter out to sea when he arrived at where the Police had told him she had fallen over. "Why didn't you hold on to her?", he cried in remorseful tones, as they tried to reason with him that there wasn't much they could have done. Having intercepted her car, they told him, they grabbed the child as she broke away from them, right on the cliff edge and lost her footing, toppling over into the sea. By now many neighbours had gathered on the cliff top in a lonely vigil that continued until darkness fell on a cold and windy winter's day. As the locals finally left the scene many were heard to ask incredulously "How could she have done this with all her money?" She had committed suicide as far as they were concerned, even though the evidence from the Gardai clearly demonstrated that she had accidentally fallen over. What she had on her mind, in her desperate condition no one would ever know now unless by some miracle the lifeboat men would find her alive. Within twenty four hours Catherine's body was washed up by the incoming tide, off the Devil's Creek, a notorious spot that had claimed the lives of many swimmers in the past. Legend had it that the place was fraught with evil, that was why the natives avoided the area and had warned tourists about the dangers of swimming there, warnings that went only too often unheeded. At the Coroner's inquest, a verdict of "Death by Misadventure" was given even though the story persisted amongst the local people that she killed herself after a row had broken out between Peter and herself. Peter and Monique were responsible for her death, the people insisted and they wouldn't be swayed from it. Others wondered, however, as to what the perception of the dreadful event would have been, had she succeeded in taking the child over the cliffs with her. It was an horrific final curtain brought down so savagely and so suddenly on Catherine Beswell so soon after the tragic end of her first husband, Clark, Peter Dunley now finding himself the undisputed inheritor of the rapidly growing group of companies.

After a short Quaker service, attended mainly by her British friends and relatives, Catherine's remains, accompanied by Peter, were flown to England for a special funeral service in her home town of Bournemouth. A cremation service followed after he had informed her family that her dearest wish always was, that her ashes should be scattered around their beloved Kerrigart Estate. Peter privately abhorred the finality of this but felt that her wish should be granted. He returned to Ireland with the urn containing her ashes, much to the chagrin and mortification of the employees of the company, many of whom would have dearly wished to have attended the funeral, but were scared it would be sinful to have been part of a service that was obnoxious to their faith, such was the teaching of the Catholic Church! Attending a funeral service was a corporal work of mercy, they were taught, as long, presumably, as it was a Catholic who was being buried!

# Chapter 38

Peter Dunley, junior, had just turned eight years of age when his father and mother, Peter and Monique were married in the Catholic church of St. Bonaventure, where the child had been baptised. Peter's mother, Nora, breathed a sigh of relief on hearing this great news. "Isn't it grand that he is back in the Faith after all those years living in sin?" she confided to family members, after receiving the invitation to the wedding. She had learned from the hierarchy, that young Peter could not make his first holy communion while his parents were not married in the eyes of the church. "Wasn't he married to a Protestant first?" Canon Jim had asked her, alluding to her son's marriage to the late Catherine Beswell. "He has led an awful life," he reminded Nora, in his usual judgmental fashion "first of all, he left the Seminary and then married outside his faith, and if that wasn't bad enough, he then went to live in sin with the French lassie, who was already married to his cousin Jerome." Nora, by now, knew differently but would not enlighten him about it. She finally interrupted to inform him that she was well aware who the father of Monique's son was, and now that they were marrying, wasn't everything sorted out, she observed. The Canon wasn't finished, however. "Did you know, Nora," he asked, "that the French woman (as he referred to Monique) had already been married in France, before leaving her husband for Jerome? You wouldn't read the likes of it in the 'News of the World', would you? And I hope you don't read that rubbish." Nora had had enough at this stage and she told him so, adding that she did not want to discuss it further. What Canon Jim didn't know yet, and she didn't reveal it, was that Father Paddy Morrissey had left the priesthood to marry Rosaleen but had been refused laicisation by the church authorities, and because of the scandal their affair was causing, they both had decided to flee the country and take up residence in the Argentine. They were by now living as man and wife with their baby daughter.

On their return from honeymoon in the United States, Peter and Monique drove up the country to visit the old couple who had so kindly taken him in on that lonely night that he fled the Seminary. When they finally found the little farmhouse, he was saddened to see that it had long since been vacated. When they told the young man in the newly completed bungalow nearby, of their business, he informed them that the old couple had both passed away some time before. Indeed, he was the nephew the old lady referred to when she provided Peter with the change of clothing on that fateful morning when he had finally discarded his clerical black priestly attire. He was bitterly disappointed not to have fulfilled his promise of visiting them before they passed on. They were the people, he always felt, who formed the bridge that took him down the path to the secular life of his new found fame and fortune. In some strange way, he felt that he should make restitution to the next of kin of that kindly old couple and when he returned to Kerrigart with Monique, he had decided that a monetary contribution to the nephew was the most appropriate way of fulfilling his wish to them. Soon afterwards, the nephew was the proud beneficiary of a sum of money that amply recompensed him for the new home he had recently built.

# Chapter 39

Within twelve months of their wedding, Monique had borne Peter two more children, in the form of a beautiful set of identical twin girls, who were named after two of his best female friends, his dutiful sister Mary Kate and his first girlfriend Rosaleen, now living with ex cleric Paddy Morrissey, who, incidentally, had secured a teaching post with a religious order in Buenos Aires. He and Rosaleen weren't even mentioned at this stage in family circles, such was the scandal provoked by his leaving the church. The locals had a field day when they first heard the news, as had members of the family, many of whom held Paddy culpable in that he had renounced his vows to run off with an attractive woman!

Although hugely successful in business, Peter's private life wasn't a bed of roses. He had received a most adverse press at the time of Catherine's death, many people still believing that he was at least partly responsible. He had, only recently survived a kidnap attempt in Wales, when a gang had tried to hi-jack his chauffeur-driven limousine as they were within sight of Chepstow racecourse where one of his horses was running. The quick thinking of the driver who veered suddenly to the right and down a lane towards a farm house where they summoned Police help saved them from certain harm. The gang was subsequently intercepted as they tried to make their get away across the Welsh border into England. Since then, he and Monique, conscious for their children's safety, had hired private security for them at the family home and for their son, Peter Jnr. who would soon be a boarder at the country's top private school. Monique had inherited Chateau Rocquefort in Normandy, the ancestral home of her late first husband which they both now used as a retreat from the stress and trauma that their enormous business interests had brought to their lives. They enjoyed the trappings that their wealth had brought; there was for example, the sea-going yacht anchored in the harbour at Sailor's Point. Both of them had recently learned to fly and they were the proud possessors of a string of the finest racehorses. However, that recent kidnap attempt had left them feeling less secure in their private lives.

Peter had by now been nicknamed 'the gold-digger' by many in the community; yet he was merely a country lad from an ordinary farming background in the West of Ireland who had made good by the extraordinary set of circumstances that had dealt him such a lucky hand of cards. How he and indeed his offspring played these cards would determine the future of what had become a vast fortune. Would Peter Dunley Jnr. and his sisters, as the true inheritors emulate their father's good fortune and shrewd business acumen? Only time would tell....


## THE END


## THE AUTHOR HAS PLANTED A NUMBER OF TREES TO MAKE RESTITUTION TO THE ENVIRONMENT FOR THE RAW MATERIAL USED IN THE PRODUCTION OF THIS NOVEL.